613 WEST JEFFERSON

Also by D. S. Lliteras:

Judas the Gentile

The Thieves of Golgotha

In a Warrior's Romance

The Llewellen Trilogy—

In the Heart of Things
Into the Ashes
Half Hidden by Twilight

D. S. LLITERAS

613 WEST JEFFERSON

HAMPTON ROADS
PUBLISHING COMPANY, INC.

for the evolving human spirit

Cover design by Marjoram Productions
Cover photograph courtesy of the author

For information write:

Hampton Roads Publishing Company, Inc.
1125 Stoney Ridge Road
Charlottesville, VA 22902

Or call: 804-296-2772
Fax: 804-296-5096
e-mail: hrpc@hrpub.com
www.hrpub.com

If you are unable to order this book from your local
bookseller, you may order directly from the publisher.
Call 1-800-766-8009, toll-free.

Library of Congress Catalog Card Number: 00-109653
ISBN 1-57174-266-2
10 9 8 7 6 5 4 3 2 1
Printed on acid-free paper in the United States

To Kathleen,
who forever believes
in my work

To Frank,
who steered this book
in the right direction

To Ken,
who found fellowship with
himself while reading this book

To Bob,
who remains steady
and always there

"*613 West Jefferson* blasts the reader into times past and present. D. S. Lliteras' unromanticized portrayal of transcendent experiences—found both in the jungles of Vietnam and a typical college town—also point to the future understanding of human experience.

"Taking us back to one of the most divisive times in our history, *613* helps us better understand the impact of war. From this battleground placement, *613* continues the massive effort of allowing us to heal ourselves and our nation, a task that has never achieved completion. Plus, through carefully crafted presentations of a mystical reality, Lliteras demonstrates how we can begin to wake up to a greater sense of ourselves. All we need to know is that such a reality exists.

"Travel with the heart and mind of war-weary Santo from the stark reality of firefights and death, to the hopelessness of a halfway house, to the glory of finding a new vision for his life. Riveting and revealing, *613 West Jefferson* is, without question, the finest work Lliteras has yet produced."

> —Ken Eagle Feather, author of
> *Traveling with Power* and *A Toltec Path*

"Lliteras' *613 West Jefferson* is a brilliantly structured, multiple-parallel novel, which explores the seedy side of returning from the war. Ultimately, *West Jefferson* is a heroic tale packed with emotional reversals and high tension—a journey into a time past, perhaps lost, but not forgotten."

> —John M. Del Vecchio, author of
> *The 13th Valley* and *Carry Me Home*

"Lliteras has written a powerful and poetic novel in point-counterpoint of Corporal Rick Santo's experiences as a Marine fighting Charlie in the jungles of Vietnam and as a brand new civilian battling a difficult homecoming that drops him in the middle of drug trafficking and promiscuous sex in a Florida college town. Lliteras writes expertly of both milieus. He's obviously paid his dues in first hand research and we are lucky as readers that he's survived to tell us this tense and harrowing but ultimately hopeful tale. His novel is head and shoulders above just about all the Vietnam War-related novels I've read, and I've read hundreds of them. Unlike most, he knows what he's doing, and that comes across on every page."

—David A. Willson, author of
REMF Diary and *The REMF Returns*

"Suffering from the shock of physically surviving thirteen months in the jungles of Vietnam, ex-Marine Corporal Richard Santo enters the drifting world of 613 West Jefferson which provides fast sex, a cheap high, and a quick escape from the world Santo is not ready to enter. Santo is slow to realize he doesn't belong because one thing he learned in Vietnam was how to survive without selling his soul. D. S. Lliteras elegantly captures the gritty reality of aimless people leading meaningless lives in a rest stop on their way to nowhere."

—Benjamin King, author of
A Bullet for Lincoln and *A Bullet for Stonewall*

"Certain numbers were the same way and certain dates and these with the names of places were all you could say and have them mean anything. Abstract words such as glory, honor, courage, or hallow were obscene beside the concrete names of villages, the numbers of roads, the names of rivers, the numbers of regiments and the dates."

—Ernest Hemingway
A Farewell to Arms

"War is your comrade struck dead beside you, his shared cigarette still alive in your lips."

—Edwin Rolfe
No Man Knows War

"Being, not doing, is the first aim of the mystic."

—Evelyn Underhill
Mysticism

TABLE OF CONTENTS

PROLOGUE
No Attachments of Any Kind ....*xv*

CHAPTER 1
Tallahassee, Florida *1*

CHAPTER 2
Search and Destroy *13*

CHAPTER 3
Florida State University *17*

CHAPTER 4
Six-thirteen *27*

CHAPTER 5
The A & P Grocery Store *31*

CHAPTER 6
Overindulgence *35*

CHAPTER 7
Ambush *37*

CHAPTER 8
"Jesus Christ, Paisley!" *41*

CHAPTER 9
LSD *45*

CHAPTER 10
Naked Bodies *47*

CHAPTER 11
"The Fine Arts Building." *53*

CHAPTER 12
War Cloud *59*

CHAPTER 13
The Briefing *65*

CHAPTER 14
Private Tortures *71*

CHAPTER 15
The Nextime Bar *75*

CHAPTER 16
Shooting Speed *81*

CHAPTER 17
"Since the beginning of time." *85*

CHAPTER 18
"Hey, G.I.!" 89
CHAPTER 19
Panama City, Florida 97
CHAPTER 20
"Sniper!" 103
CHAPTER 21
"I smell a rat." 107
CHAPTER 22
"Right on, brother." 115
CHAPTER 23
Gladys 119
CHAPTER 24
Almost Too Easy 125
CHAPTER 25
The Madness and Confusion of Battle 127
CHAPTER 26
It's Too Late 133
CHAPTER 27
"Welcome home, soldier." 139
CHAPTER 28
If It Hadn't Been for the Dying 143
CHAPTER 29
The South China Sea 155
CHAPTER 30
Impotence 157
CHAPTER 31
Utterly and Completely 163
CHAPTER 32
Sydney, Australia 171
CHAPTER 33
All Mixed Up 177
CHAPTER 34
Friends 181
CHAPTER 35
Remember When 187
CHAPTER 36
Into the Face of Reality 195
EPILOGUE
Yesterday and a Wake-up 197

the war

Striking that anvil:
wondering myself into a standstill
about the gains and losses
brought on by the war and its causes.

The sparks that fly are
preventing the calmer
aspect from shining
into the deeper shade of my being;

the sparks that fly are
the subconscious ardor,
my tempered universe,
hammered into verse

or anything; rather than be forced
to remember the back and forth
trauma—and with dread,
recall the eyes of the dead.

PROLOGUE

No Attachments of Any Kind

Corporal Richard Santo of the United States Marine Corps was drunk. He stumbled into the open bay barracks of sixty men and veered left among the two rows of racks. The sound of sleep was everywhere.

He listened to the restless movements and the irregular breaths of sleeping men as he took off his clothes. Then he eased himself into the bottom third rack, leaving his clothes where they had fallen.

There was darkness, no thoughts, and soon the blissful emptiness of sleep erased him into the relief of nothingness.

Morning always came with the intrusion of a bugle blowing reveille. Its harshness was sufficient to drive most men out of their racks.

After the bugle and the lights and the stirring of men, an encroaching pall of cigarette smoke appeared and grew steadily in the barracks. This thick smoke hung at the level of the top racks like an anxious fog that refused to dissipate. It produced an other-worldliness that made Santo pause introspectively before starting another day in a life that generally meant waiting. It was also the closest thing to an existential experience for Richard Santo, who was simply marking off his last few days in the Marine Corps; he'd just returned from a tour of duty in Vietnam.

He stretched and yawned. Then he swung his legs onto the deck and sat on the edge of his rack where he reached for his pack of smokes. The first puff activated his senses and the second, his thoughts. But introspection only carried him as far as this evening's activities of alcohol and women.

He showered, shaved, jumped into a clean uniform, and stepped into a breakfast chow line that ended with coffee. It was a quiet time of day when half-conscious eyes wandered aimlessly, though careful not to invade another man's privacy.

The completion of coffee marked the beginning of involuntary motor functions: going through the motions, getting through a tedious day of hurry-up-and-wait. It began with morning formation's dress-right-dress, with Gunny Sergeant's roll call, with First Sergeant's *Plan of the Day* announcements, and with zero-eight-hundred's salute to colors. Then the day proceeded with a maze of debriefs, physicals, out-processings, counselings, and lines—everywhere lines and formations and rows of seats.

He wandered through the day in a semi-comatose condition, knowing this was his torturous prelude to civilianhood. But it didn't matter. Because he'd already subtracted another day from the Marine Corps, leaving only four.

At the end of each day, he tried to remember the faces of the people who had spoken to him. But he couldn't. This intensified his emptiness even though he was rarely alone.

He spoke and laughed like the other Marines. But their emotions never penetrated the veneer of friendliness that guarded his deeper feelings. This inaccessibility made him invulnerable and freewheeling and respected around the barracks. Corporal Santo was considered a good guy.

He approached that day's final muster smoking the last part of a cigarette, which he flicked away with his thumb and forefinger.

"Corporal Santo, pick up that cigarette butt!" the First Sergeant ordered, his face hidden behind a clipboard.

He scrutinized the First Sergeant with an angry eye, his face hardened with defiance and his body tense with indecision. He wanted to curse the bastard but remained silent until rationality conquered his emotions.

Four days was all he had left. He was too close to freedom to ruin it now.

"Right, First Sergeant."

He found the discarded cigarette butt, picked it up, and field-stripped it. And after letting the wind blow away the fragments of charred tobacco and shredded paper from his fingers, he fell into formation where he blended into a sea of green uniforms.

The end of final muster was the beginning of time's eternal present. Not because spring was in the air and a fragrant wind blew through the leaves with a sound that cleansed one's thoughts, but because time had come to a standstill. He was free until tomorrow morning: without worries, without responsibilities, without destination. He was like a thoughtless wind blowing in all directions and, therefore, in no direction. And while the other men stormed into the barracks to shower with aftershave lotion and change into civilian clothes, he went for a walk to avoid being asked to join one of the many small groups going into town. Wanting this independence made him a loner.

His late afternoon's aimlessness was one of his joys and, as he walked, he absorbed the life around him: the sight of the shimmering leaves, the sound of the wind, the breath of clean relaxation, and the taste of dry lips. A cluster of shattered glass caught his attention. Because of the angle of the sun, he found multiple reflections of himself—jagged pieces that did not reflect a whole person. A brown eye. Some black hair. The left side of a strong chin. The profile of a prominent nose. These surface features revealed portions of a worn-out expression but lacked the depth to mirror emptiness.

After dismissing this abstract portrait, he discarded that day's past and distilled himself into nothing . . . and everything. It was like being all emotion, yet having none. He was everything and nothing and it didn't matter because he was on liberty and nobody knew anything about him.

Everybody was either in town or at the chow hall when he returned to the barracks to dress himself as a civilian. But he knew he was still an alien in the outside world and could be singled out as "one of those boys in the military." There was nothing that could be done about that. The town within reach of the base was too small for complete anonymity. And until he received his separation orders and a plane ticket home, he would have to settle for being a Marine in civilian clothes.

He hitched a ride into town with somebody driving off base. And when he entered the first available bar, he found his world intact: where money bought just about anything—with no attachments of any kind.

This time, she had dark hair. She was pretty, and he did not care where she was from or where she was going. He bought her drinks and did not bother to find out her favorite color.

They danced. They even laughed together about something. She did most of the talking, and they managed to avoid the subject of Vietnam. To his very soul, he was sick to death of hearing about the war.

These relationships quietly ended with sex, without the formality of spending the night. If she wasn't asleep, he would kiss her gently on the lips, light her a cigarette, and leave money on a table on his way out; no attachments of any kind. Then he would hit the juice joints again and drink until he began to talk. But by that time it was too late; everybody was too drunk to listen.

He drank his last drinks and howled with the other Marines until all the bars were closed and there was nowhere else to go. Then he managed to catch a ride back to the base and find his barracks: on the edge of somberness and as a stumbling shadow in search of his rack among men who had survived the same war.

He eased himself onto his rack and listened to his darkness as he wondered what the future had in store for him. He felt uneasy but he wasn't particularly afraid. Fear was something else in his life now; the war had certainly changed that. He drifted until the alcohol took over and sent him far away into a deep, dreamless sleep. And, as always, this sleep would end with another shuffling day in a life that seemed to have no end; even though there would only be three days left.

Chapter 1

Tallahassee, Florida

July 3, 1970: Richard Santo was alone.

Eight weeks earlier, he was a Marine corporal in Vietnam fighting for his life. Now he was a PFC, a "private fuckin' civilian," living in a place called Tallahassee, Florida.

The development of his detached nature had been a painful process along a perilous journey. But even to the casual observer, he was nothing more than a bewildered Vietnam veteran.

613 West Jefferson Street was an address along this perilous journey. Six-thirteen, as its inhabitants called it, was an old, single-story, wooden structure, which used to be a single-family dwelling. The place was an unsupervised halfway house for druggies, drunks, bums, and misfits living on the fringes of the hippie world. They were a sleazy lot who bordered on criminal behavior and perverted acts, but who avoided violence whenever possible.

Richard Santo parked his car and was walking aimlessly around this North Florida town when he happened to pause in front of Six-thirteen to light a cigarette. He inhaled the smoke deeply.

"Hey man, don't take life so seriously."

Santo squinted in the direction of the voice. The shadow approaching a screened door transformed into a man.

"Relax, you're among friends."

He opened the door and entered the front porch.

"Come in . . . come on . . . nobody's going to hurt you here."

He found himself among four characters: three men and a woman.

"Welcome to Six-thirteen, dearie. I'm the queen around here."

1

He looked at the pudgy guy with an empty expression.

"Don't listen to him," the woman said. "He's just a queer."

"And you, my dear? What does society call you?" the so-called queer said unmaliciously.

The woman ignored him. Then she stretched and yawned sensuously while seated on a worn-out wicker chair. She looked directly into Santo's eyes. "Don't pay any attention to him."

"Who's asking him to pay for attention?" the pudgy guy said in a suggestive manner.

"That's right, you're the one who usually pays," she said.

He smacked his lips while mentally undressing Santo. "And, in this case, I would pay handsomely."

The small group seemed hollow and tired. Santo crushed the lit end of his cigarette into an ashtray.

The so-called queer was overweight and flabby. He was extremely effeminate and spoke with an affectation. His skin was fair, his hair dark, and his eyes gray. He was partially bald and tried to conceal his bare spot with a length of hair combed over the top; it looked like a square patch of sod. He wore a pair of brown denim jeans and a wrinkled dress shirt.

The woman on the wicker chair had brown eyes, shoulder-length brown hair, and a fair complexion. Her hip-hugger jeans and white halter top revealed a lean, shapely figure. But her countenance was less than plain. Only the charm of her figure prevented her from crossing the border into unattractiveness.

The other two remained in the shadows of the porch beyond his peripheral vision.

"In or out," the woman said aggressively.

Santo hesitated. The queer laughed.

"Out," he said.

"From where?"

"Miami."

"Lord God, what are you doing in this crummy little town?"

"Looks kind of nice to me."

"But it's an awful town for us girls to make a living in," the queer said in a sisterly manner. "Isn't it, honey?"

The woman didn't appreciate the queer's remark. "It's a she-male impersonator at the Apalachee A-Go-Go."

"And she's a bitch and a whore."

"What's your name?" the woman asked.

"Rick."

The queer rose from the sofa and approached him. "Hello, Richard, I'm Kerry. And this . . . this, I suppose you're interested to know, is Melisa."

"Hello, Melisa," he said, ignoring the queer.

Kerry retreated in a mock display of brokenhearted rejection. "He's straight. You always get the good ones, Melisa." She placed a probing hand on Santo's groin.

When their eyes met, she quickly pulled her hand away, more surprised than embarrassed.

"I'm sorry, I don't know why I did that."

"Honestly, dear, keep your pants on."

"That's alright," Santo said.

"I don't know what came over me. You were just standing there and . . . well . . . I had to touch you."

"Why don't you come over here and sit by me." Kerry's heart was palpitating. "I assure you I won't apologize, Richard."

Santo leaned against the doorjamb near Melisa's chair. "What is this place?" he asked, trying to appear unaroused.

"Oh, brother," Kerry said.

"Shut up," she snapped. "Why . . . as Kerry said earlier, this is Six-thirteen: a home for the homeless, a custom fit for the misfit.

The prerequisite here is loneliness with a good dose of shiftlessness. True identity is not required. Only the willingness to overlook the sordid, the perverted, the lost, the confused. Murder is the only act considered a crime here, and morality is a civilized term that has no meaning."

Santo slowly scanned the porch. "Okay. I can handle that." Then he focused his attention on the black and white figures. They were sitting on a sofa projecting insincere smiles at him.

The black man had a coarse head of hair and a scraggly goatee. His eyes were dark, his eyebrows thick, his teeth pure white, and his large mouth severe. His other features were strong but not as prominent. A dirty tee shirt and a pair of jeans covered his powerfully built frame, and a pair of flip-flop slippers exposed a massive pair of feet.

The white man wore a cowboy hat and boots along with jeans and a tee shirt as dirty as his sidekick's. And although he was clean shaven, his gaunt figure had an overall unkempt appearance. His straight brown hair drooped down both sides of his face and framed an elusive pair of dark eyes. His nose was prominent, his mouth thin, and a constant smile exposed a set of broken teeth. Crude and blue-black in color, a homemade tattoo of a cross with the name of Jesus written below it was etched into his left forearm.

"Who are those two?" he asked Melisa.

"These two are Nat and Julian," the cowboy said. He rose from his seat to meet Santo at eye level.

"Sounds like an animal act," Santo said.

They maintained eye contact.

"You hear that, Julian?" the cowboy said.

"I'm listening, I'm listening," said the black man.

"Your compadre seems to be smarter than you," Santo said.

"Don't let his smile fool you."

4

"It doesn't."

Realizing Santo wasn't in the least bit intimidated, the cowboy offered him a friendly hand. "You're crazy, man."

Santo accepted the greeting by shaking hands with him. Then he turned to the black man, but waited for him to get up from the sofa and come to him to shake hands. When he did, it completed a small victory.

Melisa quickly established her alliance. "Would you like a beer, Rick?"

"Sure."

"How about us?" Nat complained.

"Yeah, what about us?" Julian said. But he was more worried about being left out of a beer than anything else.

"I was just checking," she said.

Nat waited for her to disappear into the kitchen. "She's a whore."

"So are you," Kerry said, "but at least she's good." He turned to Santo. "Would you like a glass with that beer, Richard?"

He sat down on Melisa's wicker chair. "A glass would be nice."

Kerry went into the kitchen with an inflated sense of dignity.

Nat pulled the brim of his cowboy hat lower on his forehead. "Faggot!"

"Screw you!"

Santo leaned back on the wicker chair. "You really like giving people a hard time, don't you?"

"We're just having fun . . . Rick."

"There's no fun in calling people names."

"What's in a name, right?"

"Yeah, we're just friends," Julian said.

"Yeah . . . like . . . Julian's the missing link."

"Yeah . . . like . . . a missing link who's going to beat on a cowboy ass."

"Just trying to make a point, man."

"Bury the point somewhere else," said Julian.

Nat raised both his hands in a display of innocence. "Hey, man, it's gone."

"Are you two always like this?"

Julian answered the question after the tension dissipated. "No, man. Only when the town is dry."

"And Tallahassee is dry, man."

"Right on," Julian acknowledged. "No drugs makes it hard on a friendship, man. And Nat here is my main man. The streets are desolate: no weed, no speed, no acid, no coke, no nothing. Something's got to give soon. People are going crazy."

The three of them slumped into another silence until music invaded the porch from one of the inner rooms of the house. Melisa entered the porch carrying beer and tossed an unopened can to Nat, then to Julian. She took the trouble, however, to open the third beer and pour it into a glass for Santo.

Then Kerry danced into the room, in drag, lip-syncing the lyrics to the song. His smile was painted with lipstick, and his head was covered with an orange wig that highlighted the five o'clock shadow on his face. His tight lavender dress accented his excess weight, and his awkwardness in a pair of high heels revealed his lack of talent. It was easy to feel sorry for him. All of them sensed his vulnerability.

They drank. They laughed. They even enjoyed Kerry's show. Then Melisa sat on Santo's lap, establishing her claim, once and for all.

As the performance continued, perspiration began to roll down Kerry's face. It ruined the heavy makeup he managed to put on before the show. At the end of the record, he threw himself into an unoccupied sofa, relishing the applause.

"Where are you staying?" Melisa asked as she wrapped an attentive arm around Santo's neck.

"I'm living in my car," he said.

"Well then, you can stay here with us."

"Or at my place," Kerry wheezed, recovering from his performance and still hoping to score.

"Nobody wants to stay with you at that dump of a hotel," Nat said cruelly.

"Where do you live, Kerry?"

"He lives at the Florida Hotel," Melisa said.

"It can't be too bad a place," Santo said in Kerry's defense.

Somehow, this sexually aroused Melisa. "It's not. Really." She got off his lap, took him by the hand, and tugged him to his feet. "Let's go for a visit. It's not far from here. We can walk and talk and . . . ." She looked at Kerry. "What do you think?"

Kerry's eyes bulged with excitement. "Who am I to question the desires of others? But I need a second to change. Don't go away." Then he vanished in a flurry of effeminate activity.

Nat was unable to contain his antagonism. "I don't believe this."

"Nobody asked you to," Melisa said.

"He's a faggot! And you're . . . you're . . ."

"Leave it alone, man," Julian said. "You've had your day with her. There are other fish in the sea."

"Yeah. Grow up," she said.

Kerry dashed into the porch, dressed in men's clothing again, and linked an arm around one of Santo's. And as soon as Kerry escorted him out of Six-thirteen into the early evening's humidity, Melisa attached herself to his other arm.

The sky was covered with an endless blanket of gray clouds that concealed the stars. The shadow of Spanish moss could be felt everywhere, and the splash of a street lamp showered the sidewalk and street with yellow light. Together they followed the intermittent lights along the narrow sidewalk of West Jefferson Street to Monroe Street. Then they steered left toward the center of town until they reached the intersection of Monroe and Tennessee Street where the Florida Hotel was located. It was the last of old downtown Tallahassee.

The square, squat, and unattractive building appeared seedy instead of old. Cracks marred its brick façade, and windows dressed with dusty drapes or yellowed shades or torn bedsheets indicated poverty's last breath. A wooden porch built to the edge of the sidewalk housed the main entrance and protected the tenants from the weather.

There were three elderly ladies and two old men sitting under the veranda's protection when they bounced across the porch and went through the main entrance. Nobody said hello.

The lobby wasn't air-conditioned, and its musty odor came from a proliferation of mildew and rot. The cranberry carpet was threadbare, and the stairway leading to the next floor creaked from the weight of its ascendants. The long, narrow hallway on the second floor was insufficiently lit, and a dirt-encrusted floor runner stretched across its entire length.

The gaiety of the threesome waned from the somberness of the hotel's interior. Kerry began to apologize.

"It's not so bad, really. You get used to it after awhile. Most of the tenants are old and quiet . . . and nice to me."

"It's fine, don't worry about it," Santo said.

They stopped in front of a door located about halfway down the passageway.

8

"Well, this is it. Home. And if not sweet," he inserted the key into the lock, "home nonetheless."

Kerry entered first and turned on the lights, leaving Melisa and Santo in the hallway. She quickly gave him a seductive wink and mouthed the words, "You want to make love?" He nodded his head and pulled her closer to him for emphasis. Then she pointed her finger in Kerry's direction as an additional offering. He emphatically declined.

"Then," she said, "as soon as we can break away from Kerry . . . you and I will . . ."

A square of light appeared on the floor through the opened door.

"Okay, you two. I can hear you whispering." Kerry stepped into the hallway. "Well, what are you two waiting for?" He ushered them into his room. "Come on in. Or is it . . . just come?" He giggled. "Oh, don't mind me. Come on, come on."

Everything in the tiny room was worn out or decaying. The walls needed painting and the cubicle needed more light. An unshaded table lamp was all the room had to offer. It produced a harsh incandescence, which created an odd assortment of shadows over the damp, stained walls. There were two doors left half-opened: one displaying a crowded closet, and the other an ivory-tiled bathroom.

Santo felt a little uneasy.

"I have to use the little girl's room," Melisa said. "I'll be right back."

"Take your sweet time, dearie," Kerry said nervously. "I believe we can manage to find something to do while you're gone." Kerry proceeded with caution after the bathroom door was closed. "Would you care for a drink, Richard?"

"Sure."

"This may not be the Taj Mahal, honey, but it does have all the conveniences that a working girl has to offer." Kerry walked over to a miniature-sized refrigerator. "Rum and Coke is all that I can offer."

"That'll be fine, thanks."

He began fixing their drinks. "You know, being straight is often a matter of degree, Richard."

"Not for me, Kerry. I'm sorry."

"Are you sure . . . you want your rum straight up?"

"Yeah."

"Suit yourself. But I hope you don't blame me for trying to change your mind."

"As long as you can stand the rejection."

"Oh, don't you know? There's a turn-on even in that."

"Did I hear something about a rum and Coke?" Melisa said, standing near the bathroom door.

Kerry handed Santo his drink. "Eavesdropping like a good little girl, weren't we?"

"A girl has to protect what's hers," she said.

"And to think, Richard, I taught her everything I know." Kerry finished preparing the other two drinks and handed one to Melisa. "Here you are, my dear."

"Thank you, sweetie."

"Now, let me propose the toast: let's see . . . to Richard and Kerry . . . and Melisa. May they become close." He winked at them. "One can only hope."

They studied each other carefully as they drank, waiting for somebody to make the first move.

Kerry set his drink on a table and lay down on the double bed. He stretched luxuriously in an attempt to appear casual.

Melisa sat on the edge of the bed next to him. And after taking a sip of her drink, she gently patted the spot beside her.

"Relax, Rick," she said. "Come over here and sit by me."

He accepted her invitation. And when he kissed her, she passionately responded, leaving Kerry frustrated among the bed pillows.

With tremendous self-control, Kerry remained calm and quiet while watching several minutes of sexual foreplay.

The couple broke their embrace and took a sip from their drinks. Then Santo placed their glasses out of the way while Melisa kicked off her shoes.

Kerry fidgeted excitedly. "Nice sequence, you two. Is there anything left for me?"

They politely ignored him as they climbed into his bed. He anxiously made room for them. Then the sound of shoes was heard falling on both sides of the bed, signifying Santo's sexual arousal on one side and Kerry's passive hope on the other.

Kerry cautiously caressed the couple. But to his disappointment, he was not included. He made several frustrating attempts, but the couple remained passively resistant. Then all the fun drained out of Kerry; he thrust himself out of the bed.

"Alright you two, have it your way. Fuck yourselves to death for all I care."

Melisa broke away from their kiss but maintained their embrace. "Don't be that way, Kerry. Please."

"Yeah, Kerry," Santo said. "It's nothing against you personally."

"Oh, sure. Placate an overweight faggot so you can use his bed."

"Wait now, you invited us."

"She invited us." Kerry pouted.

"And you resisted the whole way over here," she said.

Kerry's figure slumped. "Hell. I'm sorry. I was simply hoping, well . . . you know."

"It wasn't going to happen, Ker." She got out of the bed and gave him a sisterly hug.

"I know. I'm sorry, Richard."

"I'm sorry, too," he said.

"Really?"

"Really."

Then Santo climbed out of the bed and gave Kerry a brotherly hug. "Say . . . why don't we go out somewhere and conjure up some mischief together? Come on. What do you say, Ker?"

"That's a wonderful idea!" Melisa exclaimed with an increased desire for him.

"You two," Kerry said perceptively. "Oh, well. At least we can be friends."

"Friends," Santo agreed.

"That's right," Melisa said.

And after they snuggled up together in a three-way hug, they exploded out of the hotel room into the hallway. Then they screamed down the stairs like children and joined hands when they reached the sidewalk.

"To Six-thirteen!" one of them cried.

"To Six-thirteen!" they shouted together.

Then they marched away, locked together within a bubble of hope, on the lookout for an adventure, and always . . . always in the search for happiness.

CHAPTER 2

Search and Destroy

The elephant grass was sharp. It provided good cover but no protection. Rick's hands were bleeding because of those green blades. But the heat and the noise occupied his senses until the choppers departed. Then drops of sweat burned his fresh cuts, forcing him to wipe his face with a sleeve.

The eight men remained in their circle of silence, waiting for the enemy to make their presence known. They looked like green frogs on a waterless, razor-sharp lily pad. No one spoke.

Sergeant Russo gave the signal to move out as soon as he felt certain "Charlie" wasn't there. It felt good to release the tension of waiting. Especially since the choppers could no longer be heard.

Their short-range goal was to get away from the intensity of the sun's heat. And their long-range goal was to search and destroy and successfully steal information from the enemy. So, they pushed their way through the elephant grass into the relative comfort of shade and concealment.

Rick's breathing was already labored, making him anxious to see the break-time signal from Russo. When it finally came, everybody dropped and sat and breathlessly lit up a smoke; the patrol was going well.

Routine breaks were always quiet and thoughtful and filled with the air of gray cigarette smoke. The expression of pleasure appeared on every man's face. They knew these were the good times when the smoke smelled good.

Rick gazed at the single line formation. Its men were permanently arranged according to their job: Sunny, the point man, could see and hear for a mile; Bearcat was Sunny's back up and Rick's best friend, too; Russo, the brains, was their patrol leader; Wishbone wore first radio and was Russo's communications man; Kafka, the M-79 man, carried the heavy ammunition; Mormon rode back-up radio, but rarely spoke; and Happy walked alone as the tail-end Charlie. As for himself, he was the assistant patrol leader.

Rick knew, from experience, that their break time was about over. So, he took the deep drag that put an end to his smoke and waited.

They were still close to the bombed-out prep-sight left by the choppers just prior to their insertion. So, it was necessary to get away from that charred circle of land as fast as possible to avoid contact with the enemy.

After Russo gave them the signal to saddle up, they plowed through the bush until they became confident about their concealment and aware of dusk's approach. Then they stopped near the top of a mountain and bivouacked on its side without setting any claymore mines for security.

Russo was feeling uneasy about their surroundings and wanted the team to set up quickly for the night. His orders were: no eating or grab-assing, which meant, he was worried about Charlie smelling and hearing them.

Rick took two grenades off his cartridge belt, straightened their pins, and placed them alongside a couple of loose magazines near his backpack. Then he leaned against his backpack, took a drink from his canteen, and waited.

As soon as the darkness completely enveloped them, Rick saw a stream of blue and red tracers streak across the valley below. It was clear to him that he was witnessing a firefight by the time the sound of the rapid fire reached him. Then Rick saw flames streak across the darkness and was shocked when he realized this was a flamethrower in action. He'd never seen one used "in country" before.

He watched the flames and imagined the screams. Men were dying down there.

Chapter 3

Florida State University

Santo's eyes fluttered open to the morning light in one of Six-thirteen's bedrooms. And when he felt the warmth of Melisa's nakedness beside him, he remembered: she knew how to make love.

He yawned and stretched, but he couldn't shake himself out of his morning stupor. He rolled over and listened.

Everything was still and quiet and safe, and nobody wanted to kill him today. But the sound of small-arms fire began to invade his consciousness. He sat up. "It's over. Go away! I don't want to hear you anymore."

Melisa stirred from her slumber. "Who are you talking to?"

"Go back to sleep."

But she reached for him instead. "Come back down here with me."

He gently tucked the bed sheet around her. Then he eased himself off the mattress and pulled on his pants. The wooden floor creaked as he stepped away from her to finish dressing. But this didn't disturb her.

The room looked like the backside of a thrift shop. Mounds of old clothes lay in each corner of the room. Books were haphazardly stacked against three of the walls. And several broken bags of kitchen utensils were strewn on the dirty floor at the foot of the bare mattress. The walls were lifeless, and the windows were covered with a dirty repetition of horizontal ivory slats. The only vibrant color to the room was a light blue sheet that served as their bed cover.

He stepped out of the room with his sneakers still in his hands and shut the door behind him. Then, after a few hesitant moments in the hallway, someone carefully called out to him. He went into the kitchen and found Nat, the cowboy, sitting at the table. There was brewed coffee on the stove.

"Where's your friend?" Santo asked.

"He's still asleep. Where's yours?"

"She's doing the same."

"Coffee cups are in that cabinet."

"Thanks. Don't mind if I do."

"What happened to Kerry?"

"You tell me. What happened after that killer smoke came our way?"

Nat smiled. "Yeah. That was pretty good weed if I do say so myself."

"Was that your doing?" Santo asked.

"Not really. We have Julian to thank for that one. He took a trip into French Town last night."

Santo sat down at the opposite end of the kitchen table with his coffee. "Where's that?"

"On the other side of the campus. It's a place exclusive to Julian, on account of his color."

"I see."

"A regular holdup that place is. You can always get something in French Town if you have the proper access."

Santo raised his cup. "Thank you, Julian." Then he took a sip and set the cup down on the table.

"How was she?"

"How was who?"

"Melisa used to be my girl."

"Then you know what she's like."

"Alright. Tough guy. I don't want no trouble."

"Me either."

"Okay, then . . . we understand each other."

"So far."

"No use fighting over a woman, right?" Nat got up from the table, convinced by what he said, and poured more coffee in their cups. "This is just about the last of it. Gonna have to find a way to get a hold of some money."

"I've got a little."

"Don't tell me that, man. I'm the last person you want to know when it comes to money. Besides, you're new to all this and you've got to learn."

"What?"

"Well . . . if you're going to stay here at Six-thirteen, you've got to learn how to get money. Because you're going to run out. Hell . . . don't worry, I'll teach you."

"To do what?"

"Panhandle, con, shoplift, use . . ." he grinned. "Get the idea?"

"Use. Use who?"

"Why . . . people, of course."

"And why are you going to teach me all of this?"

"Don't worry. I ain't doing this for free. You look like a resourceful guy—I can smell it. Hell, you got my woman, didn't you?" He leaned back against his chair, feeling confident around Santo for the first time. "I'm not worried. I'll get something back from you." He took a sip of his coffee. "The length of your hair tells me you just got out."

"Yeah. From the Marine Corps. And you?"

"Army. Threw away two years of my life at Fort Bragg, North Carolina. What about you? Vietnam?"

"That's right. In the I Corps, across the DMZ, in Laos and . . . well . . . all over."

"Sorry about that."

"Nothin' to be sorry for."

"If you say so. Let's go."

They walked into a bright summer day, cut across the street, went down a short road, and walked through a parking lot that brought them to a place called the Sweet Shop. Then they entered the shop through a back door, which led into a foyer full of pinball machines with several sets of characters waiting in line in front of each machine. They were mesmerized by the bells, the silver balls, and the constant changing scoreboards.

After watching the players for a long time, Santo noticed that none of the guys were putting any money into the machines. Instead, whenever a guy got tired of playing, he alerted the man behind him to prepare himself to take over. Then they would exchange positions with a skillful maneuver and keep the ball moving on the same quarter.

Nat was waiting for a particular player. And as soon as the emaciated youth was relieved from his machine, Nat approached him. They spoke so secretively that they had to be reading each other's lips. The guy had a suspicious nature and constantly shifted his eyes in careful increments to ensure nothing escaped his attention. When he got back in line, Nat signaled it was time to go.

They walked through the main part of the shop—a curious combination of drug store, cafeteria, and hangout—and out the front door.

"What was that all about?" Santo asked.

"Just getting the lay of the land on Landis Green."

"What's that?"

"A place on campus. Sort of a park in front of the main library. Full of students, lots of drugs, things happening all the time. But not always safe."

"What do you mean?"

"Narcs, cops. The bad guys. Haven't you heard?"

"What?"

"Drugs are illegal."

They grinned; Nat's eyes sparkled with anticipation.

From the direction of their approach, two brick buildings served as a passageway onto Landis Green. It was a wide-open space covered with green grass and a blue sky. Santo was exhilarated by the energy of the students. He stopped walking to absorb the spectacle.

Landis Green was a large, rectangular lawn dotted with trees and crisscrossed with cement walkways, which led to and away from a huge marble water fountain near the library. An amazing number of students used the walkways, giving the viewer an impression of form to the disorder of changing classes. But as many students dressed the landscape with casual talk, reading, or lounging on the grass. The longer sides to the rectangle were defined by a sidewalk and decorated by an east-and-west view of the university's skyline. But clearly, the Strozier Library and the water fountain in front of it dominated the setting on the north end of this rectangle; it seemed to be the place where much of the student activity originated.

"Feels like things are happening here."

"I told you," Nat said. "Come on."

Santo sensed a wonderful mystery behind all this campus activity as they walked toward the fountain. But, most of all, he liked the unwearied faces that seemed to have no understanding of fear.

He heard the sound of rapid small-arms fire invade his thoughts; he suddenly felt out of place. When he recovered from his daydream, he found himself standing under a tree beside Nat.

There were two other guys underneath the same tree, lying under its shade. They had stringy, shoulder-length hair and wore dirty blue jeans. Nat addressed them with familiarity.

"Hank. Marty."

"Nat."

"Who's that?" Marty asked.

"One of us," Nat said.

Marty sat up and extended a friendly hand toward Santo. "Hey, man."

They shook hands.

Then Marty began to talk business. "Haven't got the best weed in town. Just the only weed."

"Does that mean you're going to shaft me?"

"Come on, Nat, you hurt my feelings even when you're kidding. Only have a nickel bag left."

"You've got to be kidding."

"Hey, take it or leave it. The Mary-Jane won't last long, right Hank?"

"Right, man."

"Okay, Rick. Pay the man."

Santo was introduced to drugs in Vietnam. So, this civilian jargon was new to him. He hesitated.

"You said you had money. I warned you, you shouldn't have told me."

"How much?"

"Five dollars."

"Here."

He gave the money to Nat while Marty reached into his pocket and pulled out a match box full of marijuana. They made the exchange.

"Great place, this Landis Green. Can usually deal openly like this."

"I noticed," Santo said. "Are you two students?"

"These two?" Nat said facetiously. "Not at Florida State . . . or any state for that matter. Hell, I don't think Marty can even read or write."

"That's right," Marty said proudly.

Nat didn't waste any time. As soon as they walked away from Hank and Marty, he rolled and lit a weed made from their nickel bag. He passed the weed to Santo after taking a long hit.

"Good . . . stuff."

They got completely stoned as they walked around the campus; they saved nothing. Their aimlessness fractured all sense of time, and their observations focused on the shadow of things.

Sounds were crystal clear one moment, then blurred the next. Sight dissipated into a kaleidoscope of colors, then shifted into the geometrics of black and white. At times, the sky was green and the leaves were blue.

"That was awfully good weed we smoked," Nat said.

"Where are we?"

"At the Student Union. Look, there's Mark Bieterman. He's screaming about something again."

"Who's Mark Bieterman?"

"An activist, you know, a socialist."

They approached the small crowd gathered around an animated figure barking enthusiastic words and challenging anyone within reach. Santo didn't listen as much as he watched the tone of Bieterman's movement and the intensity of his eyes: the movement was aggressive and the eyes were fanatical. Then he listened to the crowd: Bieterman was winning his argument by quiet default.

"I've had enough of this," Santo said. "Let's go."

"Yeah, these guys are all alike. Down with our imperialist government. Give everything to the worker. End the atrocities in Vietnam."

They roamed across Woodward Street into the newer side of the campus where the modern architecture felt stern and cold. Essentially, they had left the arts and drifted into the sciences. Santo noticed fewer students relaxing either under the sun or near the cubicle structures. Instead, there was a precise tension and meticulousness in the destination of the students.

Suddenly Santo hit the deck in response to an explosion. Then he realized he was in Tallahassee—and at Florida State University. He lifted himself to his knees, feeling embarrassed.

"You okay, man?"

"Sorry about that," he said, as he brushed himself off.

"You don't have to apologize to me."

Santo stood up. "What was that?"

"See that car over there on Woodward? It backfired. Say, man, you've got to learn how to relax."

"I'm relaxed."

"The war's over."

"No, it's not."

"It is for you."

"Yeah . . . well . . . sometimes I'm not so sure about that."

"Anything you say. You're the one with the money."

They started walking, again.

"Hey, Rick. Where are you going? Six-thirteen is this way."

"Didn't know we were going back."

"Maybe we're not."

They worked their way toward Six-thirteen: Santo taking in the sights, and Nat looking out for any opportunity to improve his material condition.

They killed the rest of the day like indifferent outsiders wandering within the din of traffic, the tremor of voices, and the drum-beat rhythm of acid-rock sounds leaking from an occasional stereo or FM radio. They satisfied their hunger, their thirst, their curiosity; they even bought a pound of coffee.

CHAPTER 4

Six-thirteen

The screen door slammed behind Santo as Nat innocently approached the figures who were waiting for them on the porch.

"What's happening, guys?"

"That's what I want to ask you," Julian said suspiciously.

"Julian, baby, you know me."

"Yeah, man, I know you."

"We bought some coffee."

"Oh, how nice," Kerry said. "Welcome back, Richard."

Melisa calmly stepped onto the porch. "Rick. I was worried about you." She went to him and branded him with a kiss. "I want you to meet someone." She turned to an attractive woman who was sitting beside Julian. "This is my best friend, Gladys."

"Hello, Gladys."

"Hi."

"And speaking of highs," Julian said, "you two . . . didn't . . . happen to run into anything while you were out?"

"If we had, we would have smoked or snorted it all before we got back," Santo said.

Julian's glare softened. Then he chuckled as if Santo had told a joke. "Man, you're a funny guy."

"Any drugs that come our way, I'm buying, okay?"

"You hear that?" Nat said. "Rick's buying!"

Julian cracked a dark smile. "You hear that, Gladys?"

"I hear that," she said.

Gladys was very thin and flat-chested. She had a washed-out complexion, blue eyes, and thin, delicate lips. Her strawberry-blonde hair was a mass of curls and split ends, which served to accentuate the carelessness of her manner . . . and her sex appeal. She wore a cool country dress without a belt and a pair of leather sandals. Her general appearance gave the impression of vulnerability, but her eyes betrayed a worldliness that could only have come from years of hard living.

Nat presented the paper bag to Melisa. "Why don't you make us some coffee."

"Why don't you make it yourself."

"Oh hell, you two. I'll make the damn coffee," Kerry said. He snatched the bag from Nat's hand and waddled into the kitchen.

"Now that we have coffee, what are we going to do about food?" Julian demanded.

"If that's our only problem, we'll get food," Santo said. "Come on, Melisa, let's buy some food."

"You've really got money?" Gladys said.

"Yeah. Why?"

"Don't waste money on food." Gladys reached into her bamboo purse and brought out a checkbook. "I can buy us food."

"I didn't know you had money, Gladys."

"I don't, Melisa. These are checks. Rubber checks. And I haven't bounced one in this town, yet. Hell, I can buy enough to feed us all for a month."

"Alright!" Julian rejoiced for the first time that day.

"And as for money," Gladys said, "that's the only thing that works . . . when buying drugs. I know someone with enough acid to take all of us on a trip tonight."

"And everybody lived happily ever after," Nat said, as he sat beside Julian. "I told you everything would work itself out, my man."

"No thanks to you," he said.

"Who wants gratitude, man. I just want to make my head right."

"Yeah . . . I love LSD," Julian said.

"Purple Dome."

"Orange Hue."

"That little dot . . . acid."

Excitement was in the air: they were getting high tonight!

Gladys rose from her chair. "Let's go shopping."

Kerry popped in from the kitchen. "I'm coming!"

Nat opened the porch door. "Me too."

Gladys linked an arm around one of Santo's. "Let's go."

Melisa grabbed his other arm. "Not without me, sister."

"But what about the acid?" Julian grumbled with concern.

"That's tonight, you fool," Gladys said. "Are you coming with us or not?"

"I'm coming. I'm coming."

The screen door slammed against an empty porch and an unguarded house. It usually remained unguarded because nobody really wanted Six-thirteen. It was the last stop on a road without a destination, a place full of human leftovers; the only direction a transient could go from here was into the streets.

CHAPTER 5

The A & P Grocery Store

They recklessly pushed the grocery cart, already stacked with meat and candy and potatoes, down the canned vegetable aisle. The six of them attended the vehicle as if it were a float in a parade. And because they looked like students, the management ignored their childish antics.

"We can't fit another thing in this cart!"

"Then get another!"

"What are we missing?"

"Beer . . ."

"And wine!"

"I'll get it!"

"Wait for me!"

"Rick, take care of the women and children."

Nat and Julian eagerly sought another cart to secure a cache of spirits. And after stopping in front of the potato chips and dips, they pushed the cart down the aisle, top-heavy with booty.

The two carts met in the next aisle for a parley.

"What next?"

"I don't know."

They carefully inspected both carts.

"Jesus Christ . . ."

"What?"

"Cigarettes!"

"The man is a genius!"

"I could have thought of that!"

"So could your mother!"

Amid the following laughter, Kerry broke away from the group to find cigarettes. "Any special flavors, gang?"

"No menthol."

"Anything with a filter."

"And several cartons' worth," Gladys said.

"A woman after my own heart."

None of them questioned Gladys's ability to pass a bad check. But if the cashier refused it at the checkout counter, they already agreed they had a lot of fun anyway. And if they actually walked out with all this stuff . . . well, then, there was going to be a big party.

Kerry returned with five cartons of cigarettes, several boxes of matches, and a half dozen packages of cigarette papers.

"Hey, papers."

"Another genius."

"It's an epidemic!"

Checkout took longer than the shopping spree, even with their enthusiastic assistance at bagging groceries. They joked and goofed around and maintained a friendly rapport with the cashier. Nat even pointed at Julian and said, "See that guy bagging groceries over there? I've never seen him work that hard in all my life."

The cashier was an amiable sort who apparently viewed the motley group as a novel change from her usual line of customers.

Gladys wrote the one-hundred-and-eighty-nine-dollar check with a steady hand. And while the others remained in an angelic tableau, she presented her identification to the store manager without blinking an eye. He initialed the check, handed it back to the cashier, and walked away.

They left the A & P grocery store, suppressing their excitement as much as possible to avoid suspicion. But when they reached the parking lot, they danced all the way to Nat's car, escorting Gladys as if she was the Queen of Sheba.

"I can't believe it! I can't believe it!"

"We did it!"

"Pass me the cigarettes!"

"I'll take a beer!"

Bags and wrappers were torn open as the groceries were loaded into the trunk of the car. And by the time Nat drove out of the parking lot, the carload of three in the front and three in the back were eating, drinking, and smoking to the sound of rock-and-roll music.

CHAPTER 6

Overindulgence

Six-thirteen had taken on an air of prosperity. Against the first shadows of approaching twilight, candles were lit and set throughout the house. The little flickers of fire filled the place with warmth by temporarily hiding the starkness of its interior; every effort was made by this hopeful group to stop the world by looking at life under the cloak of changing shadows rather than in the clarity of a steady light.

While preparing dinner, they functioned as an organic group: Kerry made the salad, Nat broiled the steaks, Melisa boiled potatoes and heated canned vegetables, Gladys set the table, Julian poured the drinks, and Santo found records to play on an old hi-fi. This cooperation inspired a sense of good will. And to their surprise, dinner was ready by seven.

The meal was devoured with gluttony and haste. And in the end, they all suffered from the pain of overindulgence, which forced them to disperse throughout the house in a gentle misery.

Santo and Melisa went to what had become "their room" at Six-thirteen. They felt like a couple of beached whales after they threw themselves on the mattress. And when they realized neither one of them had enough energy to spare the other a kiss, they laughed and settled for holding hands. The glow of the candle's single dancing lumen lulled them into a calm slumber, leaving the darkened house on 613 West Jefferson Street silent from the effects of wine and plunder.

CHAPTER 7

Ambush

Daybreak came with a mist that made Rick ache for warmth. But he settled for the smoke of his first cigarette, which lulled him into a second. He was still crouched against a tree, puffing away, when Russo's signal to "saddle up" caught him off guard. He quickly tossed on his gear and crushed out his half-smoked butt.

He knew Russo was feeling impatient about reaching their destination today . . . today, the day this patrol stood for, the day that was going to end with a night ambush.

They moved through the bush at a steady pace, being especially careful not to make any unnecessary noise to ensure the secrecy of their presence and the element of surprise necessary for a successful ambush.

They reached their destination early. So early, in fact, that this extra time threatened to give their position away with the smoke of too many cigarettes, with the sound of cellophane wrappers, and with the smell of dehydrated food. But these activities were as necessary for their survival as the strain of silence.

Rick caught himself staring at the top of his boots long after he ate. But he shook himself out of his trance with another cigarette as Russo approached him with his own canteen and a smoke. He plunked himself on the ground next to him.

"You take Bearcat, Kafka, and Mormon on the right," he whispered. "I'll take the left."

"Okay," Rick said.

"There's no indication in what general direction they're traveling. I guess it doesn't make any difference."

"Probably not."

"Don't open fire until I say so . . . no matter what direction they come from." Rick began to protest. "Unless, of course, you don't have a choice. Then do what you have to do." Rick lit another cigarette. "I want you to check every inch of the kill zone."

"You know I will."

Rick went down to the trail after their meeting was over and visually scanned its length in both directions as he thought about the absurd nature of its importance. Bearcat approached him.

"Not much of a trail, is it?" Bearcat said.

"Not much at all."

"Don't want to set up the claymores too soon."

"They don't start movement until dusk anyway," Rick agreed.

"The worst part is the waiting."

"Yeah."

Bearcat shuffled off the trail and up the slope toward their bivouac.

Rick trained his eyes eastward up the trail and followed the narrow incline until it reached a point: infinitely to the eye where his thoughts drifted into the past, into a juvenile concern over high school grades, girls and dates, money, cars . . . even a career. He wanted those things to be important, again. But he knew something in him had changed, forever.

He trained his eyes westward down the trail and allowed his gaze to travel the line that broke in a curve along the trail until it also came to a point. Then he relaxed his gaze on infinity again and drifted into a stoic trance: the kind that didn't hurt because it didn't remind him of yesterday.

"What the hell are you doing?" Russo growled, startling him from his trance.

"Wise ass," Rick snapped.

Russo was pleased with his little practical joke. "Start setting up those claymore mines."

Rick lit a cigarette. And when he turned to signal Mormon and Kafka to give him a hand, he noticed they were already laying the wire. He was glad he was working with professionals in an unprofessional war.

Once the darkness began to descend upon them, Russo hurried through one last check. Their preparation was thorough, yet simple, and that was good. Then Russo got into his position on the firing line. He peered in both directions: everything was ready on the right, ready on the left. Then he looked down at the trail just a few meters below them: nothing could get past their deadly line of fire. From this point on, maintaining silence was going to be their hardest job.

Each man created his own little world of readiness: drinking water, grenades, rifle, magazines, and M57 claymore firing devices—all within easy reach. From now on, there would be two focal points in their lives: the ambush trail below and the first explosion from Russo's claymore. There was nothing left to do but wait.

CHAPTER 8

"Jesus Christ, Paisley!"

Ghosts emerged from the night. Spirits: groping, scratching, and yawning in silence like a mime troupe in search of a bathroom, a drink, and a smoke.

Melisa stirred. And when Santo sensed her wakefulness, he whispered, "You want to get up?"

"I don't know."

"You want a beer?"

Emphatically. "No."

"Me neither." He listened to the ghosts. "How can they get up and start right into the juice like that?"

Melisa rolled over. "I don't know and I don't care."

He rolled over in the same direction and snuggled against her. He grew accustomed to the dark as he continued to listen to the others.

"That's the last cold beer," he heard Julian say.

"And it's mine," Nat said.

"Always looking out for yourself."

"There's ice in the freezer."

"Was Gladys any good?"

"Why don't you go and ask her?"

"I might do just that. Man, I've got to get laid."

"Then get laid. You know how it's done."

"I don't know what's wrong with me lately."

"You've got to hit on a chick if you want anything, Julian."

"I know that."

"Then what's this lesson for?"

"Maybe he's turning a new leaf," Kerry interjected.

"Get away from me, you faggot mother . . ."

"Ah, ah . . . be nice."

"Hand me that case of beer, Kerry."

"If you stack the beer in the refrigerator, I'll break out some ice and fill our glasses."

Julian grumbled. "Ice in beer?"

"Do you have a better idea?" Kerry said.

Reluctantly. "No."

"Then it's ice and beer, dearie. Give me a kiss."

"Fuck you."

"Fuck me if you dare."

Nat laughed.

Santo was suddenly startled by the sound of the screen door slamming shut on the front porch. He sat up on the mattress.

"Please, pilgrims, do not fear! Your savior, Paisley, is finally here!"

"Jesus Christ, Paisley! Scare the hell out of us, why don't you."

"Okay."

Paisley let out a blood-curdling scream that finally aroused Melisa.

"Who the hell was that?" she asked.

"I don't know. It's someone called Paisley."

She sat up. "Paisley! That's our acid. Come on."

They bumped into Gladys in the hallway on their way to the kitchen, where the light presented a harsh and uncertain reality—in direct contrast to the soft and reliable dream world that Gladys and Melisa and Santo emerged from. The remnants of their vulnerability still clung to them as they squinted to the light.

Paisley took advantage of the situation and sprang into a handstand to prolong their disorientation.

"Cut it out, Paisley," Gladys said.

"As one who lives with the anticipation that only seven . . . I repeat, seven Purple Domes can bring . . . how could I possibly act in any other way!"

"Seven! Paisley, you're a genius," Kerry said. He gave Paisley a warm hug.

"Seven at what price?" Gladys asked.

"At the all-time low of five dollars a hit . . . even though this town is as dry as a bleached bone. That means the acid is yours at absolutely no profit to me . . . if, of course, someone is willing to buy the seventh one for me. Gas money, that's all I'm asking for."

"Can you handle it, Rick?"

"Sure."

"Then this is the real thing!" Julian said. "You hear that, Nat? We're going to get high tonight . . . high tonight . . . forever and ever high tonight."

Nat and Julian danced in a childish do-si-do while Santo handed Paisley the money.

Paisley possessed a pair of crazy eyes, a jovial face, and a kooky disposition. He was short, stocky, and muscular. He wore a pair of scruffy jean overalls without a shirt and a pair of sneakers without socks. A hairy chest revealed itself along the bib edge of his overalls. And a thick, curly, black head of hair grew past his ears, down his face, and into a beard and mustache. His voice was deep and happy and always booming.

"Let's drop the acid and go to Apalachicola. We can trip all night on the beach . . . my treat!"

Everybody applauded Paisley's suggestion.

"Is your car still running, Nat?"

"Of course it is, Pais."

"Then you and I will drive . . . that is, unless . . ." Paisley glanced at Santo.

"That's okay by me," Santo said.

"Then let's get dressed, girls and boys!"

They dropped the acid, knowing they had a good hour before it took effect. Then they loaded beer, wine, and cigarettes into the cars before splitting the group in two: Nat and Gladys, Santo and Melisa in the Chevrolet; Paisley, Kerry, and Julian in the Volkswagen with a milk carton glued to its roof.

The moon was a transparent piece of crystal upon a clear night. It hung radiantly above the din of beach preparation. Santo was struck by its meaninglessness and, for no reason at all, sensed a calm purposelessness in his life. He was becoming familiar with this feeling and began to welcome the experience whenever it came. He never knew why or how or when it would happen but he was glad to receive the gift of its peace . . . the sense of its beauty . . . and . . .

"Hey, Rick, are you coming with us or not?" Nat shouted from behind the wheel of his car.

Santo hurriedly stepped into the Chevrolet and locked the door in a self-conscious effort to protect his private moment.

CHAPTER 9

LSD

After noticing the milk carton on the roof of the Volkswagen, a pedestrian frantically tried to get Paisley's attention as they drove by.

"Hey buddy, hey, hey . . . you forgot your milk!"

This was one of Paisley's crazy gimmicks and a constant source of laughter throughout the trip to Apalachicola.

The LSD was beginning to take effect. And as the vehicle zoomed down the road, the scenery on both sides began to break up into cosmic pointillist dots while the vehicle's motion began to resemble the sensation of flying.

The wind swirled through the open windows. Laughter became distorted. Faces turned into blends of grays in the dark with oncoming traffic lights periodically cutting them in half with white.

"Are we almost there?" somebody bothered to ask.

"Just about," somebody bothered to answer.

Melisa caressed Santo as if she suddenly discovered she was not alone. She seemed serene, and when she pressed her lips against his face, the sensation of her affection penetrated him.

Santo felt transformed . . . even transparent; the cosmic darkness infiltrated him to the very depths of his soul. The heads representing Nat and Gladys in the front seat appeared to be suspended in the thickness of the Chevrolet's dark interior, and the Volkswagen on the road ahead seemed to swerve in and out of the light.

Strange silences. Intermittent images. Mesmerizing sensations. Then Santo detected a significant change: he was alone; he had lost contact with the passage of time and space. The car was no longer moving, and all the doors were open. He was not alarmed, but he was almost paralyzed by emptiness, like that time he had sensed enemy contact while on patrol.

His perceptions reversed, and he saw himself at an angle from several feet above. His body moved sluggishly. His rifle became heavier. His mind grew distant, yet objective, curious, attentive, alert—piercing. The universe existed with or without his fear. A glimpse of eternity.

He lost another segment of time. And when he found himself again, he was standing beside the car.

With what was left of his reason, he concluded that this was not the time to suppress the acid's effect on time and space. This attitude released him from the threat of fear. And when he physically touched the car with his hands, it mentally grounded him and dissipated what was left of his anxiety so he could function in this temporary world of the strange and the new.

He heard the sound of the surf behind him. So he turned and began to walk toward the Gulf Coast. Spanish Moss gave way to open sky while pavement changed into rock, rock into gravel, gravel into sand. His sneakers slowed down his progress on the loose sand until he reached the section of the beach that was packed with moisture. Then his speed increased until he walked ankle deep into the salt water. The shoreline's wave action surrounded him . . . even disoriented him.

He stopped. This was his destination.

According to the moon, the horizon was clearly black. According to the stars, the universe was an arm's distance away. And according to himself, the earth was moving underneath him. He heard himself laughing.

CHAPTER 10

Naked Bodies

Cautious hands startled Santo from behind. It was Kerry.

"Beautiful, isn't it, Richard?"

"Yes, it is."

"Why can't it always be this way?"

"Why can't we live forever?"

"Then you have no answers either."

"I don't even have the questions."

They laughed.

"I'd like to reach out and touch the moon," Kerry said.

"Yeah . . . look at it."

"Hey, there's the man in the moon!"

"It almost looks orange."

"I want it, Richard. Like I want you."

"Don't, Kerry."

"I'd like to reach out and put the moon into my pocket."

"Friends, Kerry. We can be friends."

"I don't understand."

"You see the moon . . . the moon sees you. That's all I know, man."

Cautious hands startled both of them from behind. It was Melisa.

"I got lost," she said.

Santo placed the flat of his right hand on her face. "Are you alright?"

"I think so."

"Good."

"Let's go for a swim," Kerry said.

Melisa and Santo responded to his suggestion by taking off their clothes.

"Oh, my God," Kerry said. He began tearing at his clothes to catch up with them.

Three naked bodies found four other naked bodies knee-deep in the expanse of the black sea: they were trembling from the psychedelics.

Then they began rushing toward the horizon—joyfully, recklessly, but most of all aimlessly—against the current and into the deep. And before they knew it, there was no backward or forward, no up or down, no right way or wrong way . . . no direction at all. But they continued to run and splash and laugh and seek the comfort of companionship until . . . until Julian came to a stop. His contrasting stillness bewildered the others as they nervously rallied around him.

"What's wrong?" Nat whispered.

"Where are we?" he said.

"We're here!" Paisley shouted.

"But where's . . . there?"

"It's over . . . where?" Nat became frightened. His fear was infectious.

Suddenly, they began running in another direction. Nobody knew who made the choice or why. But they were afraid to ask the question because fear was threatening them with an answer.

They were together. That's all they knew. That's all counted. They ran for their lives.

It became a dangerous ocean, a rushing sky, and a viscous wind; the universe was moving in a multitude of directions and swallowing them up in its vastness. They were scared, and they were blind, and they kept running long after they felt dry sand under their feet.

Kerry plopped, belly down, into the sand. He was exhausted. "Not another step."

Each of the others haphazardly dropped to the ground near him, physically spent and emotionally wrought. Their naked figures loomed in the darkness; their shadows angled into the sand: they drifted into a silent alienation beyond loneliness. It began to rain.

The drops cut the horizon on a slant and gently tapped the sand.

"Christ!" Nat said. "It's raining!"

The others began to laugh.

Somberness continued to transform into happiness as two nude figures began to dance independently. And when Santo rolled onto his side to watch the silhouettes perform, he bumped into Gladys who was sprawled on her back near him.

"This is good, Rick. Thank you."

"Thank Paisley."

"He doesn't need thanks."

"Then that makes it easy."

She managed to stand up and shout into the sky. "Thank you, world!" She looked like a boy without a penis.

Paisley stopped dancing in response to Gladys's cry. Then he dropped to his knees in mock gratitude.

"Thank you, world! Thank you, Earth! Thank you, sand!"

This inspired a series of alternating exclamations:

"Thank you, sky!"

"Thank you, rain!"

"Thank you, moon!"

"Thank you, ocean!"

"Thank you, acid!"

"Thank you . . .!"

They continued these celebrations until they exhausted their imaginations.

Santo rolled onto his back and began to experience an uncontrollable tremor that shook him to his soul. He wanted to scream, but he couldn't. He wanted to panic, but there was nowhere to go. And when he realized somebody was lying on top of him, he opened his eyes and discovered it was Gladys. She pressed her lips against his and caressed him passionately. But her sexual advances seemed more like a plea for help. And after they remained entwined in a desperate embrace for the bitter period of an eternity, she stirred.

"Are you alright, Gladys?"

"I think . . . so," she answered.

"Can you move?"

"I don't know . . . if I want to." Then she passionately pressed her hips against his.

"Ohh, God, stop feeling so good."

"Why would I want to do that?" she said, as she inserted the head of his penis into her vagina and slowly eased him fully into herself. Then she moved and undulated so expertly that Santo's orgasm was almost immediate. He rolled onto his side, taking her with him.

"The sand doesn't feel as good as you," she said.

"Yeah . . . well . . . I'm sorry I . . ."

"Don't get scared . . . please. I just wanted to feel you inside me."

"Yeah . . . well . . ."

Then he exploded into another acid tremor and into his own scared world, unaware that she was fondling him, again. It was a world torn by war. A world that could not leave him alone. He heard the distant sound of choppers, the intimate cry of men, the swirling chaos of a firefight. He listened again and again and again . . . he had another erection. And when he finally felt her hand exploring him, he roused himself to his feet. Then Gladys knelt in front of him and guided his penis into her mouth. A shooting star streaked across the sky.

The LSD reached a peak intensity that made Santo experience a disjointed sense of time, each separated by a void; the confusion of leaving one moment in time and finding himself halfway through another increased his disorientation while decreasing his balance.

When Gladys finally released him, he almost fell backwards. But he regained his equilibrium and staggered aimlessly away into the hallucinogenic darkness. And aside from a few sporadic moments of awareness, Santo continued to reside in this chasm of unconsciousness until the darkness of the night began to surrender to the gray of approaching day.

Santo looked around. They were all within a few feet of each other in various states of nakedness. They appeared to be caricatures of frozen attitudes. No longer flesh, but more dense like . . . like prehistoric stones forming a ruined circle on a vacant landscape. From the deep past of an ancient life, Santo felt a curious certainty that he had once stood among these shadows. But where? When?

He saw his naked body at an angle from several feet above.

There were no words . . . just feelings. There were no gestures . . . just a little movement that eventually brought them closer together into a tighter circle. Melisa linked an arm around one of his.

Gray gave way to the sun as it began to pierce above the line of the horizon and clear the way for the blue silence of daybreak.

CHAPTER 11

"The Fine Arts Building."

They sat at a large table with hollow, concave eyes. The remnants of their breakfast were on the table.

"How did I get here?" Julian asked. The tone in his voice revealed his exhaustion.

"Why didn't you ask that before breakfast," Nat taunted.

"I was hungry, shithead."

They all giggled nervously. But when their waitress approached them with more coffee, their paranoia silenced them until she refilled all seven cups and left.

"I feel empty," Melisa announced.

"Have more pancakes, if you want," Paisley said.

"No. Thank you, Paisley. I've had plenty. I feel . . . I feel incomplete. Take me home, Rick."

"Sure."

"We can lie down together . . ."

"And let the day drift by," he said.

"That sounds like a good idea," Gladys declared. "Paisley, take me home."

Bitter resentment quietly surfaced on Nat's countenance. Julian tried to soften the blow of rejection.

"There are two sofas on the porch, my friend."

One corner of Nat's tightly closed mouth curved upward, reflecting his abject acceptance. "And there are plenty of cigarettes."

"Life," Julian agreed, "is still nothing but good. Ain't that right, Kerry?"

"As long as a person has friends," Kerry said hopefully.

"There's plenty of room on the porch, right, Julian?"

"Right, Nat."

Santo and Melisa went to the cash register to pay the bill. And when the transaction was complete, the couple beckoned the others to join them.

"How does he get to keep his woman so long?" Nat mumbled.

"Some guys must be good," Julian said. "And others . . . well . . . what can I say."

"Screw you."

Julian winked at Kerry. "Some guys have all the luck."

"Shit. Come on. Let's get out of here."

They hesitated at the glare of the day. The traffic on Tennessee Street was moderate, and the sun was still burning off the coolness of the morning. They veered left and started walking toward a large brick building with circular vaults, which made the structure look like a modern castle.

"What's this place?" Santo asked.

"The Fine Arts Building."

"It's part of the university. Let's cut through it."

They climbed several tiers of stairs, each with its own square patch of grass, and entered the building through a glass double door. A wall of air-conditioning erased the humidity.

The carpets were deep blue, the walls red brick, and the false ceiling white with soundproofed squares. The large space they were standing in was the main lobby of the School of Theatre. It also served as a hangout, a rehearsal hall, and a classroom for the theatre students. The space was vibrant with artistic activity. Santo found it fascinating.

They cut across the lobby and left the building through another set of double glass doors leading into a cement veranda and driveway.

"Is it always like that?" Santo asked.

"Always," Kerry said. "They're the chosen people. But . . . they've lost it, little by little, in a sea of envy that has destroyed any possibility of honest work. They don't know that good work breeds more good work. They'd rather have nothing. So . . . they produce nothing."

"How do they do that?"

"Oh . . . no plot, no character, no sense of rhythm . . . no talent, no taste, out of touch with reality . . . trying to compete with television and film, trying to produce without playwrights, trying to go by a book they can't read . . . begging for help, relying on slogans, insisting they're important, and not earning the right to their artistic existence."

Kerry appeared to have gotten something off his chest.

"Seems like you know something about them," Santo said.

"I used to be one of them," Kerry confessed.

"What happened?"

"You're either too good for them or . . . you're no good." Kerry hesitated. "I was no good . . . and that doesn't matter. It's the good that I cry for because it's the good that leave with battered dreams. They're the ones too good for the theatre. They're the ones that leave it all to the manipulators and to the mediocre, who, after arriving at the top, don't know what to do when they get there. The theatre? It dies right there in that lobby."

"What turned you on all of a sudden?" Nat said.

Julian chuckled unsympathetically.

Kerry turned on them with resentment. "Eat it, you two!"

"Stick it out here," Nat said. "Come on. I'll eat it."

Kerry turned indignantly away from them. "They're a couple of ignorant Neanderthals, Richard."

"And you're a faggot like the rest of them in there," Julian said, as he circled around to Kerry's right.

"That's not true!"

Julian responded to Kerry's challenge by approaching him more aggressively. Santo stepped between them.

"Alright, that's enough, you two. We're supposed to be in this together. Friends, remember?"

"He's right," Paisley said. "Listen to Rick. He's right!"

Julian's temper dissipated while Kerry's anger dissolved into a bitchiness inspired by Nat's instigating laughter. Kerry pointed an accusing finger at him.

"He started it."

"Stop it, goddamn it. I started it, okay?" And with this final statement, Santo managed to calm them down. "Come on, let's go."

"How the hell did the cars end up over here?" Julian asked.

"After that heavy acid? Who the hell knows?" Nat answered.

Their emotions were ragged, and that made them vulnerable. They knew they needed to get off the streets. They needed rest.

Santo was glad Paisley and the girls waited for them by the cars instead of adding fuel to the argument.

They rode to Six-thirteen dressed in peace and quiet because they were too beat to try on another costume. Then they shuffled into the safety of Six-thirteen and automatically went to their places: Santo and Melisa into their bedroom, Paisley and Gladys in the other, while Nat, Julian, and Kerry lounged in the porch.

Santo threw himself on the mattress and felt Melisa do the same. Then he listened to Six-thirteen's vacancy.

He felt empty, distant from the world. He didn't want to think, but he couldn't help himself; his mind raced, chasing one meaningless thought after another. He closed his eyes; he felt the glow of the midday light; he heard the sound of a clock. His sense of mortality made him feel uneasy.

Exhaustion emptied him. He stared into the relative darkness and saw himself at an angle above his physical body. He acknowledged this experience without fear.

Melisa put an end to his rushing thoughts with a caress that expressed her desire for sex. Santo was in no mood but, to his surprise, he became aroused and responded to Melisa's tender advances. At first, his behavior was mechanical. But Melisa was an expert and made his desire sincere by making love to him.

Afterwards, he drifted into a dreamless sleep, which used up the rest of the day. It was the kind of slumber that subtracted time from existence, a sleep closer to death than to life.

CHAPTER 12

War Cloud

Rick groped for his canteen and drank deeply from it. He was having a hard time staying awake. It made him angry.

He wondered if those indiscernible figures on either side of him were having the same problem. Then, in a blink, it was 0500.

The elasticity of time had accelerated his weariness. He yawned. He was glad daybreak was . . .

Rick heard a noise. He stiffened attentively. He felt the tension on the firing line as he remained frozen in position listening for Charlie.

His breathing became shallow. His eyes ceased to blink. His head tilted slowly to the right in an effort to listen. His emotions disappeared.

At an angle from several feet above, he saw his prone figure pointing an M-16 into the jungle's outer dark. He heard another sound, which drew his gaze away from himself and brought him back to his body. He thought he saw shadow movement, human movement.

He heard them again. They were moving carefully through the bush. But not careful enough to avoid death.

An explosion from Russo's claymore mine cleared the way for the others to squeeze their M57 firing devices, causing a barrage of similar explosions to clear a path of destruction. Rick heard the cry of men and the sound of gunfire, with their corresponding muzzle flashes, everywhere; he started firing his M-16 in rapid succession— he exchanged magazines twice and threw three grenades.

The enemy fired back in desperation but did little more than show courage in the face of defeat. Darkness was giving way to shadow when Rick realized his weapon was actually pointed at a silhouette. The rifle jerked softly against his shoulder; the shot was not random.

The cease-fire from Russo came as soon as the enemy's sporadic return fire ended and their own attack became ragged. Then they listened for the cry of the wounded. But death's silence was all they heard. They had done their jobs mercifully well.

Russo approached Rick from the shadows. "You and Bearcat go down there and check things out."

"Okay."

"And for Christ's sake, be careful down there."

"Yeah."

It didn't take long for them to reach the trail but, when they did, he slipped onto his rump into a puddle of blood. It was a grizzly sight: body dismemberment, attitudes of death, and the human mud of dirt and blood. He remained seated as he studied a decapitated body that was plastered against a tree. He was a bit overwhelmed by the grotesque results of their work.

"Are you alright, Rick?"

He looked at Bearcat, noted his outstretched hand, and accepted it. Bearcat pulled him to his feet.

"Yeah. I'm alive." And when he heard the others approaching the kill zone, his mind became clear again. "But I'll kill the first bastard who starts clipping earlobes or collecting teeth."

"Hell, our guys don't do that stuff."

"I swear to God, I will."

"Okay. Okay." Bearcat hesitated. "I'll . . . go check and make sure." He scampered toward the approaching men.

Rick took off his bush cover and became a respectful sentry over the dead; he was determined to prevent any unnecessary mutilations.

"Goddamn, we blew the hell out of them!" Kafka shouted. He danced around like a marionette, unsure about what to do next.

"See if there is anyone alive."

Kafka grinned uneasily as he looked around at the remains. "Can't be."

"I know. Check anyway."

"Sure. Sure." Kafka regained his composure. "That's why I'm here."

Rick watched him pick through the remains, noting that a hospital corpsman would have softened the activity with compassion. But corpsmen were in short supply these days, and recon teams had to make due with guys like Kafka who knew more about first aid than the average Marine. Besides, compassion was not a good trait for a professional soldier who had to be sure there wasn't an unexploded grenade pressed under a limb, waiting to release a deadly explosion.

Rick lit a cigarette and sighed: who was he to judge?

Kafka was a good man, a hardened bush Marine with three six-month extensions to his credit. He was tall and thin and so pale that the brutal Vietnam sun constantly burned his complexion. He was probably twenty-two years old. But the deep-set lines extending from his worried mouth and his harassed eyes erased much of his youth.

Russo stomped past them gnawing on a cigar.

"We've got to hurry and get out of here," he said. "Search and be quick about it!" Bearcat extended a handful of documents to him before he had a chance to take another puff from his cigar. Russo eagerly snatched the papers and almost devoured his cigar as he scanned them. "Good. Good! Rick, here, take a look."

"What have we got?"

"Look. An NVA colonel."

"Yeah . . . shit . . . a real soldier."

"Looks like some kind of consolidation going on near Quang Tri. Damn. I wish I knew more Vietnamese. What do you make of it?"

"I don't know, Sarge."

The two of them studied the documents while the others continued searching through the bodies and the debris.

Suddenly, an explosion sheared off a tree at mid-length, creating a huge wooden lance suspended in the sky. Then it plummeted, impaling the earth with such force that it seemed to replant itself. But the tree began to lean, then came crashing down. Several more explosions hit the ground so violently that they shook Rick off his feet.

Russo's cigar fell from his mouth as he rolled toward Rick with astonishment. "What in God's name . . ."

"We've got to get the hell out of here, Sarge."

"No shit!" Russo barked. He stood up, stuffed the documents into his right leg pocket, and started up the trail with an exaggerated gait that said: this way, right now, like this. They followed him east, up the trail.

Rick was surprised to hear the distant sound of a chopper. And in a short time, a Cobra roared past them. He was already grateful for the air support he knew they were going to get—he heard the Cobra fire one of its rockets. When they reached the top of a hill, Rick came alongside Russo, who still had the handset to his ear. He began to repeat the message he was receiving for Rick's sake.

"Better get the hell out of there. You have a battalion of NVA on your tails. I'll try to hold them back as long as I can. Run. Over."

Russo shook his head with dismay. "Geronimo, this is War Cloud. Roger. Out."

There was nothing more to say. They knew it would be useless to ask for an extraction: any LZ would be too hot.

"No use wasting any more time," Rick said.

"Right. Let's move out."

They were fighting for their lives. One false move, one wrong decision, minutes lost in any direction would mean a fight to the death. The enemy was approaching them like a life-threatening storm at sea, leaving them no choice: they had to run before the wind.

Speed, not concealment, was what they desired now. But the trail was growing smaller and soon there would be no trail at all. Then the bush would impede their progress with its claws of branches and vines and thick brush tormenting them. But they had no choice. They had to bulldoze their way through: cursing and pulling and yanking themselves clear, and away from the enemy.

CHAPTER 13

The Briefing

Santo's body shivered from abuse even though the evening was humid. He pulled a portion of the bedsheet away from Melisa and draped it over himself. And as he tried to fall back to sleep, he heard the door slam on the front porch. He listened.

"Where have you two been?" a probing voice asked.

"Here and there and everywhere."

It was Paisley.

"But we got results."

And that was Gladys.

Santo sat up attentively. The bedsheet fell to his hips.

"Someone turn on the lights around here."

Paisley could be heard prancing with excitement throughout the front part of the house.

A slice of light shot past the open bedroom door and reached the foot of Santo's mattress. It gave the bedroom form.

"Where's everybody?" Paisley demanded.

"Over here and over there," Nat said. "Hey, what have you got in the bag?"

"Hands off, bozo. You too, Julian."

"Don't be so touchy," Kerry said.

"Okay, everybody together. Where's Rick and Melisa?"

"In there."

"Follow me."

They tramped down the hallway.

Shadows violated Santo's bedroom, then disappeared with the flood of a harsh overhead light. Melisa stirred from the injury of this invasion and sat up blurry-eyed. Both of them tugged at the bed-sheet to secure a modest wrap around themselves: Melisa up to her breasts and Santo around the waist.

"What the hell are you guys doing?" Melisa said.

"Not to worry, my dear. Mr. Paisley is here."

Santo was beginning to enjoy this crazy man's antics. He leaned back on both elbows.

"Gather round, my children, and you will hear about how all your troubles are soon to disappear." Paisley stood holding a brown paper bag while Gladys, Nat, Kerry, and Julian sat around the edge of the mattress surrounding Santo and Melisa.

"Miss Gladys and I, while you peasants wallowed in slumber, took it upon ourselves to plan for our future . . . your future. Now, you may be wondering what that future is . . . or, what it has in store for you . . . well, your future . . . is in this bag." Smiles began to appear in Paisley's audience. "Ahhh, I see that you all have already guessed what it is that I have in store for you."

Julian was unable to contain himself any longer. "Are you going to make our heads right, or are you going to talk about it all night?"

"Patience, my dear fellow. Don't you know that the element of anticipation is almost as important as the act?"

"Man, what are you talkin'? Open the damn bag," Julian said.

Paisley winked at Gladys. "Peasant."

He reached into the bag and presented each item with dramatic flair: a little cocaine, a little speed, a hypodermic needle, an elastic band, and finally, a nickel box of weed. The group was ecstatic.

Julian picked up the hypodermic needle. "A set of works! Damn! You're a genius, man, a genius!"

"Thank you, my dear fellow. It just takes a little spooky dust . . ."

"And a little cash," Gladys said. She kissed him on the cheek.

"Thank you, my dearest."

Nobody asked Paisley where he got the money.

They migrated into the kitchen, leaving Santo hopping into his pants and Melisa furiously arranging the bedsheet around the length of her body.

Everybody waited breathlessly. And when Paisley was ready, he stood before them holding a square piece of mirror on the flat of both hands with seven long lines streaked across its surface. Gladys stood beside him with a dollar bill rolled tightly into a short green straw.

"Seven equal parts to get us started tonight." Paisley carefully laid the mirror on the kitchen table and took the rolled dollar from Gladys. "I'll take the first snort." He grinned. "Just to make sure this isn't poison."

He bent over the glass, aligned the green straw with the end of the first white streak, and inhaled the line of cocaine into his right nostril. The rush of the dust and the burn to the sinuses temporarily blinded him as he stomped away from the table sniffing and snorting.

"Good . . . good stuff," he managed to say between nasal gasps. "Next."

Each one of them went through the same performance. And after the rush of their highs leveled off, they became quiet and grateful and immersed within a sea of cigarette smoke. Nat began a verbal banter with Julian.

"Good stuff."

"What have we got next?"

"Can't you ever enjoy what you've got?"

"A man's got to survive."

"How high does your high need to be, man?"

"The highest of highs. That's my career."

"Suck on this if you want a career."

"Now why are you doing me that way for?"

"Because it's the right thing to do."

Santo went into the front porch where Paisley was already occupying one of the sofas.

"Have a seat," Paisley said. "We've got to make plans."

Santo lay down on the other sofa. "For what?"

"For tonight."

"Business?"

"Drug business. Can you handle it?"

"That depends."

"On what?"

"The type of drug."

"Weed."

"How much?"

"Eight kilos."

Santo sat up. "Where?"

"Panama City. You interested?"

"What's in it for me?"

"What do you want?"

"A stash for myself."

"We all get that if we succeed."

"Who's we?"

"Nat and Julian will be in on it."

"I'm in if we don't use my car."

"No problem. It's Nat and Julian in one car, me and you in the other. That splits the load in half, just in case."

"In case of what?"

"What do you think?"

"Ahh . . . yes . . . drugs are illegal."

Paisley grinned. "You're crazy. I like that." Then he became serious. "This business . . . it's going to make for a long night."

"Is that the reason for the speed?"

"You've got it." Paisley stood up. "It's time to make plans. Come on. Let's pick up those clowns in there and get down to business."

They brought Nat and Julian out of their euphoria and into the caper while sitting at the kitchen table. The others remained on the periphery but were listening attentively to Paisley's briefing. Kerry occupied himself by making coffee, Gladys by rolling the nickel box of weed into five healthy jays, and Melisa by getting dressed and putting on makeup.

The place was a bar where U.S. Navy divers hung out. The time was supposed to be late that night. The owner wanted cash upon delivery. Paisley indicated he was only a middleman and the cash he had hidden inside Six-thirteen's broken washing machine was not his money. This was not organized crime. He was emphatic about that. The weed they were buying was North Florida home-grown; simply, Bay County locals trying to make a living.

As the briefing proceeded, they smoked all the Mary-Jane and drank Kerry's coffee.

Paisley was careful to point out that Florida cops were tough and, if they were caught, these cops would show no mercy: they would be charged as drug dealers working for the mob and they would end up as somebody's boyfriend in Rayford State Prison. No one questioned the risks.

Santo lit a cigarette and posed one question. "What happens then . . . if we get busted tonight?"

Paisley also lit a cigarette. "Then . . . it's every man for himself."

Julian nodded insightfully.

"Anyone have a problem with that?" Paisley waited. "Then it's settled. We all know who drives and who rides where. Nat, you follow me all the way to the parking lot of The Down Under. That's the name of the bar. It's across the street from a small naval base called the Naval Coastal Systems Center. If you blink your eyes while driving by, you'll miss the place. Anyway, once I make the exchange, half goes to you, Julian, and the other half goes to you, Rick. Then we split back here in different directions."

"Sounds good to me," Nat said enthusiastically. "When do we start?"

"As soon as I get the rest of the money. Rick, I want you to come with me. You two sit tight until we get back."

"Is there any beer left in the refrigerator?" Julian asked.

"Sure," Kerry said.

The girls occupied the vacated kitchen chairs, prepared to stay there until Paisley and Santo returned. Kerry served everybody a beer. And as they began to drink under the quiescence of a single light bulb, the screen door in the front porch slammed shut: Paisley and Santo were gone.

CHAPTER 14

Private Tortures

The hump had become a mindless effort to push one foot ahead of the other. A brutal pace had been set for five long hours.

Rick began to believe he was part of something inhuman. And he was beginning to believe he wasn't tough enough to keep up when he almost ran into Mormon; Russo had ordered a break. He continued walking until he reached Russo's tired eyes and realized he'd been facing his own private tortures. They sat quietly for a short while until their strength returned.

"What a way to make a living," Russo said.

"Yeah."

"We'll sit here and wait 'til . . . near dusk. Then we'll hump it until it's too dark to go on. It's going to be port-and-starboard watches tonight and the smoking lamp is out until I say so."

"Okay."

Rick stood up and went to pass the word.

The heat was unbearable throughout most of the day. And the inert wall of leaves surrounding them prevented any possibility of a breeze. There was nowhere to go, nothing to do except stay alert and conduct frequent radio checks.

Perspiration plastered Rick's shirt to his chest as he leaned against his backpack in a helpless stupor. He peered at Bearcat, who was sitting next to Sunny. Bearcat raised one of his massive hands and waved limply at him. Rick smiled at the big bear as he thought about Guantanamo Bay, Cuba, where they first met.

Cuba. Not too unlike the hellhole they were in right now, except for the war. Living there in garrison was a hot, monotonous affair with very little to occupy a man's mind away from home.

Bearcat managed to overcome some of this monotony by tilting two giant speakers together in teepee fashion and slipping his head between them while lying on his top rack dressed in a pair of skivvy shorts. He hibernated like this every day, groaning to the sounds of Bob Dylan.

Amazingly, nobody paid any attention to him, no matter what the hour. He was entertainment for the drunks who stumbled into the barracks at all hours of the night and a noise buffer for the ones already asleep against those same nightly drunks.

The solid rock of Bearcat Bradly kept the barracks' tension down to a manageable level. His presence even discouraged any physical violence—limiting self-destruction to the vomit of overdrinking, to an occasional threat of A.W.O.L., and to the cursing of God himself.

Rick shifted his gaze to Sunny.

Sunny removed his bush cover, revealing his blond head, and ran his fingers through his wet, matted hair. He pulled out a canteen and took a long drink, enjoying the sound of the gurgling water. He lowered the canteen, feeling relieved yet exhausted from the heat, and sat staring at his boots with his canteen still open. Sunny was totally defenseless against the sun and his extremely fair skin always turned cherry red when it was left uncovered. His eyebrows and mustache were also blond, his eyes blue, his lips thin, and his head skull-like. He never thought about anything other than women and booze and wore a Catholic crucifix around his neck to make sure he was safe.

Rick's mind drifted.

The endless day was finally drawing to a close. Rick had written a poem and considered sending it to his ex-girlfriend. But he crumpled the poem in his hand and buried the wad of paper in the dirt beside him.

He heard Russo giving orders. It was time to saddle up.

CHAPTER 15

The Nextime Bar

The humidity was stifling. Santo looked at the clear sky for relief among the stars and the moon. "Hot night."

"Yeah," Paisley said. "Hope it doesn't get hotter."

They stepped off the curb, crossed the street, and jumped into Paisley's Volkswagen Bug.

"Where are we going?"

"To the Nextime Bar. Ever been there?"

"No."

"It's a dive. But the people are friendly, the talk is cheap, and the beers are a quarter."

The Volkswagen jerked out of its parking spot and chugged to its destination. Santo always felt like he was in a coffee percolator every time he rode in one.

Paisley parked in a shabby, irregularly shaped lot behind the bar. They got out of the vehicle and crunched through the broken glass and pavement as they weaved around the back of the building through a narrow alleyway, which led to a busy thoroughfare in front. They hung a right at the sidewalk and proceeded toward the main entrance of the bar.

The sidewalk felt too narrow beside the threatening four-lane traffic on Tennessee Street. Santo felt the drag of each passing automobile on the nearest lane and became a little apprehensive about their proximity and speed. Paisley opened a glass door leading into the bar and invited him to enter first.

The cool darkness and the relative quiet of the place made them feel as if they had walked into a comfortable vacuum. Paisley pointed at two empty bar stools.

"Over there, Rick."

They sat down at the horseshoe bar and ordered a couple of drafts. Then they sipped their beers slowly while becoming acclimated to their surroundings.

The most distinctive feature of the place was the friendly vocal chatter devoid of background music. Santo liked the subdued quality of the establishment: the sound of billiards balls clicking and banking off the sides of the pool tables in back, and the low murmur of a television above the cigarette smoke.

"Who are we looking for?" Santo said, as he lit a cigarette.

"For that man right there."

Paisley indicated the direction with a glance.

Standing within the frame of a half-door that led into the pool hall was a dark man with two distorted arms sticking out of a plaid short-sleeved shirt. He waited patiently with a cue stick held vertically beside him until a barmaid set a draft on the narrow ledge of the half-door. Then he paid for the draft, gulped it straight down, and left about an inch of beer on the bottom before thumping the glass back on the ledge. He turned his head slightly in Paisley's direction and passively blinked his eyes.

"Let's go," Paisley whispered.

They walked into the pool hall where the billiard balls were heard slamming into the pockets more clearly. Smoke hung thickly below the low-level lights that illuminated each table. And cigarettes dangled from mouths taut with eight-ball concentration.

Paisley remained a respectable distance away from the man, waiting to see what his next move should be; the man was still involved in a snooker game. Paisley leaned against an unoccupied table as Santo stepped beside him. From there, they watched the progress of the game.

Santo made an uneasy observation about the man they were supposed to meet: he looked sleazy.

"What's the story, Pais?"

"It would look suspicious if he walked away from a money game. That would be a forfeit on his bet."

"Understand."

"You see that door over there?"

"Yeah."

"That's his office. As soon as the game is over, that's where we're going."

"What's his name?"

"Mr. Manford . . . and, don't forget the mister. He's funny that way."

"Okay. But I still don't understand why you wanted me to come along with you."

"Hell, look at him," Paisley said. "Would you trust that snake alone? Besides, I wanted someone along with a little common sense, just in case . . . you know, in case I went down on a bust or something. This way you'd know what's going on: where the money came from and where the drugs go. Believe me, you don't want to piss these people off. And don't ask me who these people are, Rick. You really don't want to know."

"Why do I have to talk to him at all?"

"Because if you have to come back here without me, he won't acknowledge your existence otherwise."

"What if you and I don't come back?"

"Don't even think that, man. Once we walk out of here with the other half of the money, one of us better come back with his merchandise. And just in case you're wondering, it's already too late for you: he knows your face; now he knows who you are."

"Thanks. Buddy."

But before Santo could elaborate on his displeasure, Paisley alerted him with a nudge. "Let's go."

They walked toward an office at the back of the pool hall with Mr. Manford following in their wake. Then he unlocked the door and led them into his tiny office.

They spoke carefully.

"Who's this?" Manford said, referring to Santo.

"A friend."

"I don't trust friends."

"Then don't make him one," Paisley said.

Manford didn't like Paisley's curt statement. But before he was able to respond, Paisley softened his remark with: "Mr. Manford."

The glare in the man's eyes changed from lukewarm to cold. He reached into his desk, pulled out a tightly rolled wad of bills bound by a thick rubber band, and handed it to Paisley.

The amount of money made Santo feel uneasy. But he remained expressionless even against Manford's hard scrutiny.

Paisley snapped the wad's rubber band to attract Manford's attention.

"Don't you trust me?" Manford wheezed.

Paisley smiled incredulously. "In this business?" He began counting the money.

"It's all there." Manfold pursed his lips. "Carol is expecting you at the Down Under."

"I know," Paisley said, as he continued his tally, making Manford wait beyond his patience.

"Okay, Mr. Manford. Same time, same station tomorrow?"

"Correct."

Paisley led the way out of the office and through the back door into the shabby parking lot where the Volkswagen was parked. They both lit a cigarette.

"You can't take any shit from those guys," Paisley said, as he exhaled the first drag of his smoke. "If they think you're afraid, they'll consider you weak . . . then eat you alive."

"I know. So, why do you deal with . . . with that kind of element?"

Paisley was amused by Santo's choice of words. "Element?" He searched for the proper answer. "It's exciting. I like being on the edge."

"But if you fell off the edge, he would kick you while you were down."

"Then I have to make sure he knows that I would take him down with me if he tried."

"Theory doesn't always work, you know."

"I never theorize, Rick. I always live as if I'm going to die tomorrow. I just don't give a damn . . . and, I make sure they know it.

"Are you a veteran?"

"Hell no," Paisley said. "But it's okay if you are."

Santo was amused by Paisley's indifference. Then he wondered how he understood dying tomorrow without the experience of war.

"Come on. This place gives me the creeps."

They crossed the parking lot and got into the Volkswagen.

"What now, Paisley?"

"We get high, of course."

"Of course."

Paisley started the percolator and began driving back to Six-thirteen to prepare for tonight's undertaking. Santo sat quietly, spinning with dissociated thoughts about the war and the risks of this evening's adventure. Then he shifted his attention upward and discovered the moon floating peacefully in the dark sky. A wave of tranquillity invaded his senses and dissolved his inner turmoil; the decision to participate in this scheme had been made.

He shifted his gaze and greeted the stars, their presence a reminder of the randomness to all things. He settled into the noise of the automobile's engine and let it drown out his thoughts into the comfort of thoughtlessness.

CHAPTER 16

Shooting Speed

Paisley and Santo discovered five bored figures loafing on the edge of anticipation in Six-thirteen's seedy front porch furniture when they returned from the Nextime Bar.

"Hello, handsome," Kerry chimed. "We missed you."

Nat was unable to contain himself any longer. "Well, goddamn it? Now what?"

Paisley disappeared into the kitchen and returned with his brown paper bag of speed and paraphernalia. "It's time to get high."

"I hear that," Julian said, always enthusiastic where that was concerned. This was his one clear direction in life.

Paisley handed the bag to Julian, knowing this would happily occupy him. "We'll hit the road for Panama City as soon as you make everybody's head right."

"Anything you say, my man." Julian rung his hands like a fly. "Somebody lock the front door." He set the bag on a wooden side table, then placed the table in front of a wicker chair; he sat down. "I need cotton, a candle, a spoon, and a glass of water."

Kerry quickly located and presented the items to him.

"Thank you, Kerry, baby."

Julian lit a short candle seated into the neck of an empty wine bottle. Its flicker seemed to give meaning to the lives of Six-thirteen's inhabitants.

He removed the contents from the bag: a cellophane pouch of amphetamine pills, a hypodermic needle—commonly known as "the works"—and an elastic band to tie around the upper arm to bring up a vein.

Julian's eyes sparkled. This was the only activity that brought calmness into his being.

He dropped two pills into the spoon, squirted water over them with the syringe until they were submerged, then cooked the ingredients over the flame while stirring it with a matchstick until the pills dissolved. Then he laid the spoon on the table, tossed in a tiny ball of cotton, and submerged the tip of the needle into the liquid, using the cotton as a filter. He carefully pulled the plunger out and drew the liquid into the works.

Nat stepped forward. "I'm first." He picked up the elastic band and tied it around his upper left arm. Then he slapped his forearm until he saw a fat vein. "There's a good one."

Julian handed him the works.

Nat placed the needle parallel to his left forearm alongside the enlarged vein. Then he pushed the point through the skin and into the vein. He retracted the syringe's plunger until he saw his blood mingling with the solution, then slowly pushed the plunger in. The rush up his arm made him let go of the works in ecstasy, leaving the syringe stuck in his vein. He staggered a bit and accepted Julian's assistance into a chair.

"Wow, man, what a rush."

Julian took hold of his arm. "Hold still." Then he untied the elastic band and pulled out the syringe. "Looks like we're all getting high tonight."

Within the hour, that statement had become a fact; they were filled with the well-being associated with shooting speed. Suddenly, they had all the time in the world: no topic of conversation was too trivial, no observation was too small. Their bodies felt balanced and their movements graceful. Everything was beautiful. Love was tangible. Laughter and hugs and incessant chatter made immortality feel good.

At first there's a rush, then there's the speed of a high, followed by the buzz of a plateau when shooting speed. It was during this plateau when Paisley regained control of himself and encouraged those who were involved in that night's operation to do the same.

After the others came into focus, danger's realization crept into them, dampening their humor and darkening their souls. The contagion spread to Kerry and the girls; even the candle went out, leaving them among static shadows—they were washed away with a lamplight. It was 9:00 P.M.

CHAPTER 17

"Since the beginning of time."

Santo waited on the sidewalk in front of Six-thirteen while Paisley retrieved the other half of the money from the broken washing machine, while Nat pulled on his cowboy boots, while Julian gathered several packs of cigarettes to see them through the night, and while Melisa furtively approached him from behind and linked her arms possessively around one of his. This habit of hers was beginning to make him feel uneasy; he did not like smothering women.

"Be careful, Rick," she said in a wifely manner.

"Don't worry about me."

"I'm glad you're with Paisley."

"Yeah . . . well . . . I'm sure Nat and Julian will do just fine."

"I fixed up our room while you were gone."

He maneuvered his arm out of her stranglehold. "Be sure none of you say anything about this to anyone."

"Don't worry. Gladys and Kerry aren't leaving the house either tonight."

"Good."

"We're even locking the front door to keep out the street."

"Oh? I didn't know you could do that here."

"Sometimes. But regimes don't last very long at Six-thirteen."

"Regimes?"

"Yeah. You see, anarchy usually prevails, making this place nothing more than a flophouse. Then, every so often, people like yourself and Nat and Paisley come through that door and merge into a cohesive force . . . almost like a family . . ."

"That acts like a regime."

She nudged him affectionately. "Go on. Now you're making fun of me."

"I'm sorry."

"I know. Anyway . . . it doesn't take a genius to see when it's happening . . . and when it does, Gladys and Kerry and I jump on board for the ride. It's . . . a hell of a way to make a living, isn't it?"

"What happens to the other people?"

"You mean, the ones still on the street?"

"Yeah."

"Word gets out that Six-thirteen is occupied. So, they stay away. They know nothing lasts. They know it isn't worth a fight . . . for control. They know that you and Nat and Paisley and Julian are . . . strong. So, they wait for the inevitable."

"Which is . . ."

"You know. The infighting that weakens the family until . . . well . . . until each of you start peeling off in separate directions. As soon as the streets smell the break-up, they move in like roaches, turning Six-thirteen back into a nest. Then anarchy prevails, waiting for the cycle of control to begin again."

"How long has this been going on?"

"Jeez, where have you been?"

"What?"

"Haven't you heard? Since the beginning of time. As soon as something isn't owned, as soon as it becomes everybody's . . . it becomes halfway. And it decays with abuse until there's nothing left."

"Because nothing's for free."

"That's right. You know that. I know that. Everybody here knows that." Then she pointed in the direction of the campus. "But those people over there with the brains don't seem to know that.

So, we hop on and take the ride for as long as it will go, knowing that nothing can come of it, knowing that someday there will be an unpaid bill hopelessly overdue."

"That's a hell of a scenario."

She shrugged her shoulders. "It's the truth. And we better hope we're dead or too old to care when that day comes."

"That's bleak."

"That's why I, almost never, talk about it with anyone."

"Alright, you guys! Kiss and trade hugs," Paisley said. "It's time to go." And as Paisley went to his car, Santo followed his instructions with a candor he didn't have before.

Paisley had the car started by the time Santo poked his head through the opened side window. "Are we ready?"

"As we'll ever be."

Paisley placed a brown paper bag on the unoccupied front seat. "Here's our half of the money." And when Santo heard Nat start up his Chevrolet, he took that as his cue to get into the Volkswagen.

Paisley eased away from the curb into the street with Nat following close behind.

CHAPTER 18

"Hey, G.I.!"

Their movements were swift and silent into the approaching darkness. This was a critical hour for them, and great care had to be taken to conceal themselves from the enemy. The NVA probes were going to be out looking for them tonight.

The silhouettes in front of Rick moved skillfully through the bush as if they were traveling through space and time in slow motion. And as the bush swallowed them up, the trees looming over them emphasized their isolation.

When they finally had to come to a halt because it was too dark to go on, Rick sensed the tension from the other exhausted statues. The very ground beneath them was going to be their beds, and the act of releasing themselves from the weight of their backpacks and cartridge belts was all the luxury they could expect. There would be no unnecessary preparation for their nocturnal existence: no food, no bedding, no smokes.

Rick steadied himself for the potential terror of this night. He knew there were no plans beyond concealment. And if anything went wrong, all they could depend on was their meager arsenal of weapons and their mental discipline. There was no need to assign watches; who could sleep tonight?

Rick nestled himself as comfortably as he could and leaned against his backpack to gaze at the piece of sky that peeked through a narrow opening in the jungle's canopy. He focused his attention on the only star available; it took him to a brighter, happier time full of anticipation:

"And remember, let's not pick up the first thing we see when we get into town," Bill said.

"Why not?" Phil asked excitedly.

Bill peered at him as if he were an insect. "I know these things, that's why." He continued to strut about the barracks uncomfortably in an effort to get used to the civilian clothes he was wearing.

Phil danced around with so much excitement in his eyes that Rick thought they were going to pop out of their sockets if the threesome didn't leave soon. Phil caught hold of Rick's shoulders and shouted into his face, straining with anticipation. "I've heard that if you couldn't get laid in Olongapo within an hour, you weren't worth a fuck!"

Only Phil was amused by his raw wit. But they all laughed.

They were greeted by a beautiful sunny day, which overwhelmed their happy hearts. They headed for the naval base's main gate like three musketeers with Phil's excited chatter serving as a sound track.

Rick suddenly felt exhilarated when he realized he was not anticipating a sniper's bullet, making him aware how very far the war had taken him away from home.

He joined Phil and Bill in a new round of laughter after they passed through the main gate. They were free! Truly free!

The foot bridge leading into town was their final transition from battlefield to silk. There, they faced a barrage of children beggars and leftover streetwalkers, which they diplomatically repelled. And when they reached the other side of the bridge, Olangapo, Philippines, revealed itself under a golden sun. They were drunk with joy.

Then a second barrage of unfamiliar faces seemed to be waving at them through every door and window on the strip: half-dressed prostitutes, pimps in Bermuda shorts, elderly ladies with groceries, and truckers unloading beer. Curiosity pulled them in every direction. But they managed to stay together as they passed by the Texas Bar, the Stork Club, the Bar California, the New Yorker—bar joints—as far as the eye could see.

Phil giggled nervously as they quickened their pace. "Kind of neat, huh?"

"A little weird, if you're asking me," Bill said. "But wide open, don't you know?"

"Suits me just fine," Rick said, as he observed four morning-girls release themselves from the safety of their saloon entrance to greet them on the sidewalk. The girls wore seductive smiles and suggestive poses. And their Tagalog chatter confused them as the ladies herded them into the coolness of an empty bar, then escorted them to a table where they were greeted by an obese bartender with a cheerful voice. "You want drinkie?"

"Let's have three beers," Bill said. "And something here for the ladies."

The girls responded with such enthusiasm that it made Rick feel uneasy about the safety of his wallet.

The woman sitting next to him seemed to have read his mind. "We no steal from you. What's your name?"

He relaxed a bit. "Rick. What's yours?"

"Aurora." She hesitated for a moment as Rick gazed into her dark eyes. "You from the Navy for permanent at Subic Bay?"

"No. The Marine Corps," he said. "On permanent station," he lied.

Her large eyes were beautiful.

"Let's dance," she said, as she took him by the hand.

She led him to a jukebox, where he started to take out some money. But she surprised him when she told him to put it away.

He admired her compact body as she deposited a coin and began selecting her numbers. Her shining black hair was pinned to the back of her head, but long wavy strands wandered sensuously near her delicate ears. She had smooth, bronze skin and genteel features. But her youth was betrayed by the worldly look in her eyes. His admiration shifted back to her lithe figure dressed in brown bed slippers, tight-fitting, pastel-blue knit pants, and a semi-transparent white blouse that revealed the outline of her breasts.

She pulled him toward her and they began dancing to the rhythm of the low-playing music. Her soft body melted onto the hard contours of his muscular frame that seemed to become more rigid because of his uncontrolled arousal. He began to feel self-conscious.

Again, she read his mind. "Nobody looking. Nobody care."

"I don't care either," he lied.

She smiled as her hands roamed his body. And he winced at the soft pleasure, which he had not known for some time. As they continued dancing in a manner that shielded their intimacy from the others, he became lightheaded with passion while her expert hands continued to roam for areas of pleasure to inflict erotic pain.

"Give me five pesos," she whispered.

"Why?" he asked in heat.

"Do you like me, Rick?"

"Sure, I like you."

"You want to go upstairs?"

Rick hesitated. But she fondled and caressed him into submission.

"Come. Five pesos is nothing. I like you."

He half-believed her because five pesos was nothing. But he also suspected that she was virtually giving herself away to him because he looked like an easy mark—a green American with great potential.

He peered into one of the dark corners of the bar and discovered he was being watched. She noted his discovery. And with a final tug, she said, "Pay him and we go upstairs. Go. Pay him. I promise no regret."

She reached for his wallet in his back pocket.

"Alright," he said nervously, as he drew out a five and handed it to her.

She broke away, momentarily, leaving him exposed. But only the bartender laughed at Rick's embarrassing condition.

When she returned, she grabbed one of his hands and led him up a flight of stairs into a dark hallway of doors. He was relieved when she opened the first door on their right and motioned him to go into the room; it wasn't too far from help.

"You from Vietnam . . . too long, yes?"

"Yeah," he said, as she shut the door behind him.

"No sweat, I take care." Then she started unbuttoning his shirt.

He stood there in total submission gazing about the room. It wasn't much.

There was a bed against the wall and a white plastic shade, cracked with age, drawn over a narrow window. On the opposite wall stood a nightstand with a pitcher of water and a wash basin, a tattered length of fabric brushed aside like a shower curtain to reveal an empty closet with two wire hangers, and a chair. An ashtray and a box of kitchen matches were on the floor beside the bed.

The subdued light filtering through the window-shade softened the room's stark appearance.

He felt her hands roam over his chest.

"You are very handsome," she whispered seductively. Then she undressed herself.

Rick admired the fullness of her breasts. And when she peeled off her pants and exposed the dark triangular patch of hair between her legs, he could not contain himself any longer; he disrobed without taking his eyes off of her.

For a moment, they stood apart admiring each other. Then she reached intimately for him.

Their lips touched before their bodies met in a passionate embrace, their tongues darting frantically at each other. She broke away from him, momentarily, and with one of her hands still in his, she locked the door. Then she led him the short distance to the bed.

He climbed onto the bed while she positioned herself beneath him and, with an expert maneuver, she helped him enter her. The soft wetness inside her readily accepted his length and engulfed what was left of his senses. Nothing else mattered.

Rick exhaled the smoke from a freshly lit cigarette. The room had grown darker.

The nap they had taken felt good. He shifted to his side and touched Aurora's shoulder to feel her warmth.

She rolled toward him with sleepy eyes. "Five pesos good?"

"Five pesos very good," he said.

"You my man from now on, right?"

"Sure. I'm your man from now on."

He didn't tell her that from now on meant five days. He took a drag from his cigarette and offered it to her, which she accepted.

He wished he could tell her how little time they really had together, but he knew that would be dangerous. He watched her take a drag and allowed the tiny glow of light, a cigarette point in the dark, to draw his focus back to the star in the sky . . . to the reality of the here and now . . . to the reality of the flame of pain he was experiencing in his legs, thighs, and hands . . . to the reality of unfamiliar voices calling in the night.

"Hey, G.I."

"Hey, G.I.!"

"We going to kill you, G.I."

The omnidirectional voices were foreboding and as real as the burning pain in his thighs, which further disoriented him. Only his mental discipline kept him from giving away their position. And when he rubbed one of his thighs, he discovered there were insects crawling all over him.

The feeling of being eaten alive brought him near the edge of panic as he frantically brushed them away. Then he lifted his buttocks off the ground, using his hands and feet for support, after he realized he was sitting on a disrupted ant bed. Something had to be done soon or he would go mad.

The sinister voices continued to accompany their probing, as the enemy searched freely in the darkness for them. Rick remained in his four-point position, hoping this would all go away like a bad dream. But it didn't.

"Hey G.I., we going to kill . . . you!"

He knew he had to move. There was no choice in the matter. He decided to leave everything where it was and roll some distance away. He knew if they found him, he was dead. But he had to take that chance.

He waited for the voices again, knowing they would be preoccupied with their dramatics more than their search at that moment. He waited. The inflammation of the ant bites was beginning to numb his legs, back, and hands.

A diabolical shriek cut through the density of the bush like a knife, slashing him with fear. He wondered what private hell the others were going through.

"G.I., where are you?"

Rick snapped to his right in a quiet roll. Once. Twice. But he dared not a third time.

"No use, G.I. You die!"

He knew this distance would have to suffice. Then he turned his concentration back to listening; the pain had reduced the abilities of his sensory perceptions to one at a time.

The following silence was deafening. The enemy was playing a new game.

Rick shifted carefully onto his side to take the pressure off his burning buttocks. He clenched his fists and concentrated on not scratching. But the pain was driving him mad. He began to cry.

He buried his head in one of his arms and wept quietly as he waited for someone to put a bullet in his head.

CHAPTER 19

Panama City, Florida

20 West, the two-lane road leading into Blountstown where they would turn south on Highway 231 for Panama City, was dark.

Santo lit two smokes and handed one to Paisley. This act served as a vocal catalyst for Paisley. His harmless chatter lasted until they reached Blountstown, where they stopped for gas and Coca-Colas. Then paranoia infiltrated his behavior, infecting the others.

The harsh fluorescent lights of the convenience store, in contrast to the comfortable obscurity of the unlit road, made them whisper and measure their movements. They appeared stiff and out of place, and they left as quickly as possible.

When they finally reached Panama City, Florida, it was 11:30 P.M. Paisley made the necessary turn onto Highway 98, which took them easterly across town and over the Hathaway Bridge. They passed the small naval base and made a left onto 757. A minute later, Paisley drove into the parking lot of their destination: a bar called the Down Under. Nat rolled up beside them and cut off his headlights.

Paisley released both hands from the driver's wheel for dramatic emphasis. "Okay Rick, let's not waste any time."

They got out of the car while the other two sat tight. Julian simply rolled down his window and passed the other half of the money, also in a brown bag, to Santo. Then he followed Paisley around to the back of the building, where they approached a weather-beaten door. But before Paisley had a chance to knock on it, somebody unlocked the dead bolt and swung the door open.

Santo felt ill at ease and began to feel the weight of the money.

They entered a dimly lit room, which served as a storeroom and as an office. And after shutting the door, a woman gracefully escorted them to a cluttered metal desk. The atmosphere reeked of mildew.

"You're here early," she said.

"Couldn't be helped."

"And someone new, I see."

"Is that a problem?" Paisley asked.

"Not your usual standards."

"I'm growing confident in my old age."

"Let's hope confidence isn't synonymous with recklessness."

She was British. Her refined manner, along with her proper accent, seemed incongruous in these surroundings. She was tall, thin, and had a fair complexion. And although she was plain, she was not unattractive. Her light brown hair was shoulder-length and pulled to one side behind her left ear in a loose pony tail. She wore a long-sleeved white blouse with a pair of pressed jeans.

When Santo presented the money to her, she finally smiled. This illuminated her eyes and revealed a startling intelligence. She reached into one of the bags, pulled out the money, and thumbed the corner of the bills like a deck of cards. "Do I need to count this?"

"Only you can answer that question," Paisley said.

Her eyes twinkled. "You always say the right thing."

"I aim to please."

Her eyes dulled to normalcy. "Quite." She pointed to four burlap sacks. "There's your merchandise. I suppose you need to be quick about it."

"What about the coke?"

She presented a cigar box to him. The lid was secured with two thick rubber bands.

"Do I need to check this?" he asked.

Her eyes lit up with pleasure, once again. "Even I would feel compelled to raise the lid. It's from a different supplier."

"Then please, do me the honor."

She unsnapped the rubber bands and opened the box, disclosing several cellophane pouches of cocaine. Santo became uneasy.

Paisley picked out one of the bags and opened it. He stuck a dry finger into the white substance, then placed it on the end of his tongue. "Tastes good to me."

"When shall I see you next?"

"Not sure I'm doing this next."

"Pity."

"Is that some sort of invitation?"

"Perhaps."

Paisley smiled. "I guess it's worth a tank of gas to find out."

"As long as it's round trip."

"That was understood."

She appeared to be pleased. "Good." And as Paisley re-secured the box, she addressed Santo. "I suppose you're his relief then?"

Santo shook his head. "Not likely."

"I see." She dismissed him. "Well then, Paisley . . . until we meet again."

Santo shot a heated glance at Paisley as soon as they were in the parking lot.

"You lied to me, goddamn it."

"About what?"

"The deal was for weed only."

"That was your assumption. Besides, drugs are drugs, man."

Santo was furious. Cocaine was serious business. But it was too late to do anything about it now. And by the time he reached Nat's car and transferred two of the burlap sacks to Julian through the window, he was resigned to the situation. Julian sensed his wariness, however, and probed him.

"That was easy, man."

"Yeah." He felt compelled to warn him. "Paisley's carrying a load of cocaine."

"Where did that come from?"

"I don't know. But it's enough to put us in jail forever."

"Christ."

"So don't let yourself get arrested, no matter what."

Nat leaned across Julian's lap in an effort to get as close as possible to Santo. "This changes everything."

"No shit."

"It sure does take all the fun out of this joy ride," Julian said.

"I should leave the bastard and come along with you two . . . but I won't. You guys better take off. Remember, we don't know each other. That should make it easier for you two if . . ."

"Hey, man, these people aren't stupid," Julian said. "If we get busted, they'll be able to figure out that we're in it together."

"Then look at it on the bright side," Santo said.

"What's that?"

"You're black. You're going to fit right in with the prison decor."

"Then I'm going to make sure we get the same cell, so you can appreciate the interior design." They chuckled as they clenched their fists together in a brotherly affection. "You be careful, my man."

"Yeah, sure," Santo muttered. "Now beat it before we start drawing attention to ourselves."

Nat started the Chevrolet and backed away. Then the car skidded softly off the oyster-shell-covered parking lot onto the road's blacktop; its headlights pierced the darkness when Nat finally turned them on.

Santo began to feel paranoid as he watched them drive away. The threat of arrest would have been less likely without the cocaine since law enforcement agencies focused their efforts on hard-core drugs. This made marijuana busts incidental as they went along their merry investigational way. But that was no longer the case.

The utilitarian purpose of the speed was unnecessary now; there was enough adrenaline pumping through his veins to keep him awake for a week. He didn't remember getting into Paisley's Volkswagen.

The flash of the oncoming traffic headlights jarred him out of his pensive state. He glanced at Paisley, who seemed to know where he was going as he drove across town through unfamiliar streets.

Santo began to relax and feel the stillness within him until he became centered. He tasted the dryness of his throat, touched the fabric of his surroundings, and smelled the freshness of the air.

He knew something was going to go wrong tonight. But there was nothing he could do to prevent it.

His last premonition occurred while on a patrol tagged with the call-sign, "black hawk." Santo saw death after they were shot-out of two hot LZ's. So, when scuttlebutt brought him news about an available dive billet within their battalion, he double-timed over there.

The dive locker was near his company area, and the sergeant-in-charge who recruited him was a friend. This released Santo from regular patrols, including *black hawk's* next insertion attempt.

"Don't go!" he wanted to scream. "I see death!" But they would have to ignore him.

He was crippled with vertigo by the hollow screams trapped inside his skull, which forced him to stay in his rack on the day they were to leave. There were many choppers flying out that morning, but he knew which chopper was carrying *black hawk*. He closed his eyes and broke into a helpless cold sweat: *black hawk* went out; nobody came back.

Santo opened his eyes. No escape this time. But he did not see death. He stared at the oncoming traffic. He knew something was going to go wrong tonight.

He was ready . . . to deflect the oncoming danger.

CHAPTER 20

"Sniper!"

Daylight awakened Rick from his unexpected sleep. But he didn't sit up until somebody nudged him.

"We're moving out," Mormon whispered. "Say, what's your gear doing over there?"

Rick rubbed his eyes. "Ants."

"Whoa. You okay?"

"Think so."

Rick stood up, as Mormon moved on to pass the word. Then he went to his gear and inspected the area. The ants were gone as if it had been a nightmare. He put his gear on and picked up his rifle. It was time to go.

The hump started at a breakneck pace that knocked the wind out of him. Rick didn't have time to confide in Russo before they started, so he didn't understand the purpose of this push. It was too early for this kind of speed since the new day's surroundings were dangerously uncertain.

A scream, up ahead, confirmed his apprehensions and brought the team to a halt after a hundred meters or so. It was Sunny, the point man.

He rushed to his assistance. And when he saw the open sky behind Bearcat, he realized Sunny had fallen off some kind of ledge. Russo was already preparing a rope to send down to him.

"Don't say a word," Russo mumbled. "It's my fault."

Bearcat lay on his belly and looked down on Sunny. He'd been caught by a huge tree limb. And although it saved him from falling to his death, he was straddled on the limb writhing in pain like a broken-winged bird. Bearcat cupped his hands over his mouth like a megaphone. "Hey, Sunny. Sunny. How're you doing down there, guy?"

"Christ! I've busted my balls! Get me out of here!"

"Coming, Sunny. We're coming!" He turned to Russo. "He'll be alright."

"Of course he'll be alright," Russo said, as he started to lower the rope.

A ricochet pinged off a tree. They all hit the deck.

"Sniper!" Bearcat yelled. "Sniper!"

"Where the hell is he?" Rick shouted.

"I don't know, I don't know!"

"Get me the hell out of here!" Sunny screamed in a panic. Another bullet smacked the dirt wall in front of him. "Oh God, oh God, I'm going to die. Will you guys get me the fuck out of here!"

"Heads up, Sunny. The rope's coming down."

They ignored the continued sniper fire as they lowered the rope; speed was the only defense against him.

Rick, Russo, Bearcat, and Kafka worked in plain view to rescue Sunny while both radiomen sat behind their rifles searching for the sniper; Happy stood watch to protect their rear from attack.

Sunny stretched out his arms to grab the rope and quickly secured it around his waist. And when another bullet smacked the side of the mountain a few feet away, it no longer bothered him. The odds were in his favor: VC Charlie was a terrible shot, and he had a rope around him.

"Coming up, Sunny!"

Rick saw Sunny's relief when the weight was taken off his groin.

"I don't think I've got to worry about birth control anymore," Sunny said, as they hoisted him up. He had wild eyes and an evil grin when he finally reached the top. "What took you guys so long?"

"Had to have breakfast first," Bearcat said affectionately.

"Okay, let's get the hell out of here before that sniper finally gets lucky," Russo barked. "Besides, every damn VC in the area knows where we are now. Saddle up!"

"I guess the sniper finally figured he was wasting his ammo," Sunny said.

"It would have been a wasted bullet if he dinged you, anyway," Kafka interjected.

Laughter erupted.

"I said cut the grab ass and saddle up!" Russo shouted. "You feeling alright, Sunny?"

"Sure, I'm okay."

"Good. You take it easy for awhile. Bearcat. You're point man."

"Right."

"Are we ready to go, Rick?"

"In a second," he answered, as he supervised the last moments of organizing gear, rope, and men.

"We're getting the hell out of here today, no matter what. Our mission is complete. Besides, we're no good anymore since everybody knows where we are. We're going to hump for a couple hours to get to a good LZ and call in the choppers. Let's move out."

Rick sensed a surge of energy: they were going home.

CHAPTER 21

"I smell a rat."

The nonstop trip back to Tallahassee was uneventful. Paisley took a longer route back by staying on Highway 98 East all the way: first going southward through Port St. Joe and Ward Ridge, eastward through Apalachicola where the highway also became 319, then northward through Carrabelle and Crawfordville before reaching Tallahassee; this route roughly paralleled highways 10 and 90 East.

They were about twenty-five miles north of Highway 20 that went through Blountstown. Avoiding that road on the return trip was the safer thing to do; none of them wanted to be busted in Blountstown.

Santo was no longer angry, and Paisley ceased to be apologetic. They quietly chain-smoked as their neutrality remained a constant throughout the return trip. That is, until they approached Tallahassee from the South on 319 where it became Crawfordville Road meeting Woodville Highway.

Santo resisted the impulse to turn around when he noticed Paisley's change in behavior.

"What is it?" he asked.

"A cop car," Paisley answered.

"What do you think?"

"I'm not sure. Coincidence, I hope."

"Drive carefully."

"I am."

"And quit driving so slow."

"Stop worrying. I'm not going to give them any excuse to pull me over."

Paisley suddenly stepped hard on the accelerator.

"What are you doing?"

"Turn around!"

The patrol car's flashing blue lights said it all.

"Shit!"

"Hang on!" Paisley said.

Paisley had the gas pedal to the floor. But the Volkswagen Bug rattled instead of roared. The little vehicle whined as if it was going to explode, but Paisley continued to push the engine to its limit. There was no possibility of outrunning that squad car on a straightaway; a series of maneuvers and turns was their only hope.

Paisley hit their first turn so hard that everything loose in the cab shifted and bounced in a fit of confusion as the vehicle almost rolled over. Santo stabilized himself by spreading both hands against the dashboard and both feet on the floorboard like a mad spider.

"We haven't got a prayer in this car!"

"I know that!" Paisley said. "Hold on!"

He steered the car off the road, plowed into an open field, then veered toward a wooded area. This maneuver slowed down the squad car, giving them enough time to stop at the tree line, disembark with their cargo, and break off on foot in separate directions.

Santo held the burlap sacks tightly under each arm. He zigzagged wildly among the trees until he felt the darkness swallow him up. Then he stopped and quickly scanned the area behind him. He saw two uncertain beams of light probing the darkness.

Santo quickly looked around and discovered a shallow knoll to his left. He scooped out the fallen leaves at the base of it and placed both sacks into the depression. Then he pushed the leaves back over them. He stepped back and inspected the area: it was the best he could do.

In an effort to prevent any noise from drawing attention to him, he didn't run. He carefully backtracked around the two flashlights instead. It was a daring choice to make. And he hoped the officers weren't considering this method of escape. They weren't: the flashlights continued their search straight ahead.

He felt a measure of relief, which he quickly suppressed. He knew there was no time for that. Until he was sitting on the porch at Six-thirteen, he was not safe.

He pressed on relentlessly, moving through the brush like a bush Marine running for his life: he half-expected to hear small-arms fire and choppers overhead.

He stopped. He listened. He pressed on. This behavior continued throughout the night until he reached a recognizable part of town. He regained his bearings and headed directly for Six-thirteen. It was close to daybreak when he arrived at the front door.

The lights were out. But he entered the porch without hesitation and immediately sensed a darkness charged with anxiety.

"Richard? Is that you?"

"Yeah. Is that you, Kerry?"

He heard sighs of relief all around him.

"Man."

"Can we turn on a light now?"

"No. Are you crazy?"

"Did Paisley make it?" Santo asked.

"We all did. You were the last."

He recognized Julian's voice and sat on the sofa beside him. "You mean . . . you and Nat almost got busted, too?"

"Sure did. But we didn't lose our car. We got away clean. What took you so long to get back?"

"I was lost. I don't know this town very well yet."

"You've got to be tired."

"I'm beat. But I couldn't sleep if my life depended on it."

"Hell, me neither."

Everybody began to giggle nervously and with relief, as if a floodgate had been opened. Then flashes of light appeared haphazardly, producing orange embers floating in the dark along with the smell of cigarette smoke.

Santo felt an anxious hand on his shoulder and placed one of his over it. He knew it was Melisa.

"Thanks a lot, Paisley, buddy, pal," Nat said tauntingly.

"Sorry, guys. I did it. I know." He almost sounded sincere.

"Where were we, Paisley, when all hell broke loose?" Santo asked.

"We were near the Leon County Fairgrounds."

"And which way did you come into town, Nat?"

"Off Interstate 10 going East. When we took the exit onto Monroe Street, they were waiting for us. What're you getting at, Rick?"

"At what you said: they were waiting for us."

"That can't be . . ."

"Shut up, Paisley. You've lost your credibility."

"Don't be so hard on him, Rick," Gladys implored.

"Alright, alright," he relented.

The group became silent for a few moments, allowing the darkness to wash away some of the tension. Then Paisley penetrated the quiescence.

"We've got the merchandise stowed in the attic. I think it would be a good idea to hide the rest of the stash up there, too."

"Yeah, that's true. But I don't have it," Santo said.

Paisley almost suffocated with an anxiety attack. "But . . . what . . . you can't . . . shit!"

And when Santo felt he had tortured him long enough, he added, "But don't worry. I buried the sacks under a pile of leaves. The stash should be safe for the time being."

He saw Paisley's shadow rise from its seat with relief. Dawn was beginning to spill through the jalousied windows.

"I'm glad you got back safely, Richard."

"Thank you, my dear Kerry. Say, why don't we all go into the kitchen, turn on a light, and make some coffee. It's morning. There's nothing to worry about."

They wandered into the kitchen like uncertain phantoms, turned on the overhead light, and set the coffee percolator on the stove. Friendly conversation ignited and filled the kitchen with warmth. And after the coffee was poured, they focused their attention on the stories concerning that evening's escape. Nat and Julian began their tale first.

"We didn't think we were going to make it. But my expert driving saved us," Nat boasted.

"Only thing he forgot to tell you was he shit in his pants first," Julian said.

Everybody laughed. Their comedy act was just the thing they needed.

It had been just as close for Nat and Julian, but they had a faster car and a better driver. They managed a clean getaway on the outskirts of town. Then they cut directly for the center of town and zigzagged their way to Six-thirteen as fast as possible without drawing attention to themselves. They realized time was against them; the longer they were on the streets, the worse their chances were for escape. They parked the car at Southgate Apartments' parking lot down the street and calmly sauntered into the safety of Six-thirteen, each carrying a burlap sack.

Cigarette smoke filled the room as they drank their coffee. Gladys nestled herself against Paisley while Melisa and Kerry attached themselves to Santo.

Paisley's story was an impressive odyssey that came to a climax when he made physical contact with one of the cops. He knocked the officer unconscious with a savage blow to the jaw and ripped the badge off his shirt to validate his story. Everybody's mouth dropped in amazement when he plunked the badge on the kitchen table.

"Crap. That's nothing to be proud of," Santo said. "In fact, it's stupid."

"What the hell was I supposed to do, let him arrest me while holding a cigar box full of cocaine?"

"You could have left the badge behind. Now we've got an angry cop out there looking for us."

Santo's rationale sullened everybody's attitude toward Paisley, again. Even Gladys pushed herself away from him.

"Alright. I'm sorry . . . again!" Everybody waited for more. "I'll even cut you all in on an equal share of the profits. It's the least I can do for the trouble I've put you all through."

"Okay, Paisley," Santo said. He knew this was no time for serious in-fighting. That would get them caught. But he was glad they had cleared the air a little. "We won't say anything more about this. What's done is done. Everybody agree?"

"Of course, macho man," Kerry said, as he poured coffee into their empty cups. A new warmth filled the kitchen. Gladys even reclaimed her position by Paisley.

Then Santo told them his escape story. And when he was finished, a sense of loss prevailed. Everybody knew the other two sacks of marijuana had to be rescued. But nobody volunteered to say it.

"Okay, guys, this was all my fault. But I've also lost the most." Paisley raised his hand with one finger showing. "I lost my car." He displayed his second finger. "I've lost my freedom now that the cops know who I am through my vehicle registration." Then his third finger popped up. "But worst of all, I may have lost four kilos of prime weed." He lowered his hand. "I'm not going to continue with this and bore you. But I am going to ask you for a favor." Everybody shifted uneasily in their chairs. "Hear me out. You especially, Rick. I can't stay in this town anymore. But I don't have the money or the car to do anything about that. We've got to get that weed you buried so we can complete the deal tonight. It's all or nothing, Rick. I told you that yesterday. I'm dead if I walk into the Nextime Bar with a partial delivery. These people don't listen to excuses . . . not at all." He pointed a finger at Santo. "They'll be looking for you, too."

Santo slumped in the face of this truth; he even finished Paisley's line of thought. "So you figure we get the weed, make the deal, divide the money, and you get out of town with Nat and Julian."

"It's the only car we've got."

"What makes you think I want you along with us?" Nat said.

"Because it's always dangerous if anyone from a group is left behind to get caught," Paisley said.

"I smell a rat," Julian growled.

"Not me!" Paisley countered innocently. "But you never know. You've got to be careful about this kind of stuff."

"I'd like to go to Atlanta," Gladys said hopefully. "I'm getting tired of this little hick town, anyway. Would that be alright with you, Nat?"

He shrugged his shoulders. "What the hell, the more the merrier, I guess."

"We could go together, Melisa," Gladys said. "I could get us work. I know a good pimp up there." Melisa glanced at Santo, feeling guilty. "Oh, come off it, honey. Rick's been around. He knows you've done tricks. Right, Rick?"

He didn't answer.

"Then it's settled," Gladys said. "You're coming with us when this is all over."

By remaining silent, Melisa agreed. The glitter in her eyes had gone out.

Santo wanted to comfort her. But he knew she would misinterpret his gesture as a commitment to her. Kerry clearly read the situation and came to their aid by offering Melisa his sisterly affection. She was grateful.

The speed they had taken was completely out of their systems and, coupled with coffee nerves, they were beginning to suffer from the drug's depressive aftereffects. The world began to look and feel ugly. Window shades and Venetian blinds were drawn closed against the reality of the day, and the kitchen light was turned off.

Seven empty shells wandered restlessly through the darkened house like solid shadows until their emotional and physical helplessness finally paralyzed them.

Time ticked by slowly as the day burned away. Six-thirteen fell into a state of dormancy.

CHAPTER 22

"Right on, brother."

". . . which brings us right back where we started," Santo said. "The cops were waiting for us."

Four solemn figures sat at the kitchen table: Paisley fretfully bit his lower lip, Julian agitated a smoldering cigarette, Nat thumped a repetitive tattoo against the table with his index fingers, and Santo stared into a cold cup of coffee. The others were still asleep.

"How long have you known that English lady in Panama City?"

"No. It's not Carol. I promise you, Rick."

"We don't have many people to choose from."

"Then it's got to be Manford," Paisley insisted.

Santo settled back in his chair. "Okay. Then it's Manford. What are we going to do about it?"

Paisley shifted uneasily in his chair. "How the hell should I know?"

"Yesterday you knew everything, man," Julian said irritably.

"Is that the guy we're making the deal with in town?" Nat probed.

Santo shook his head. "Yeah. He runs the Nextime Bar on Tennessee Street."

"I know the place. Is that where you two went the other night?"

"That's the place."

Nat also settled back in his chair. "Okay, so?"

"So," Paisley interjected, "if we're smart . . . we don't mess with him."

"We've already proved that we're not smart," Julian declared as he crushed out his cigarette.

"You can say that again," Santo said.

"This guy Manford is connected, man," Paisley finally announced. "We don't want to play with him. We want to get what Rick buried out there and we want to finish this deal, clean. Don't try to figure these guys out. And for God's sake, don't try to get even. Everything is going to be dangerous enough as it is tonight."

Nat lit a smoke, inspiring the others to do the same. "I agree. I'll be happy if we can just finish the deal." But the word "connected" rang in their ears. Paisley was a liar.

"Now that this is settled, how do we do this tonight?" Paisley nervously persisted.

Julian stood up. "Give it a rest, man."

"That's easy for you to say. You're not on the run!"

"I said back off, man!"

"Remember, it's important that we all get out of this. Remember," Paisley said.

"Is that a threat, you little son of a bitch?"

"Easy, Julian," Nat finally said. "Sit down. And Paisley . . . you don't know when to shut up, do you?"

"Hey . . . look . . . Rick could end up in a lot of trouble, too, you know."

Julian pointed a threatening fist at Paisley. "I don't know about you, man." He wanted to hit Paisley, but he managed to maintain control of his temper. "But I'll stay in this for Rick's sake."

"Thanks, Julian."

He winked at Santo. "Right on, brother."

Nat stood up and went to the stove to make more coffee. "Alright now . . . is the air finally clear in here?"

"As clear as it's going to get for me," Julian qualified.

"Well, then . . . let's stop screwing around and decide what we're going to do tonight."

"I agree," Santo said.

They all volunteered to go to the fairgrounds that night to recover the four kilos. But only three had to go: Paisley, because he knew where the incident took place; Santo, because he was able to pinpoint the exact spot; and Nat, because it was his car. Julian insisted on going because they were partners and because they needed a lookout during the pickup. They also needed another strong arm; there was no telling who they were going to encounter at the Nextime Bar or on the fairgrounds.

With that realization, they armed themselves with the only weapons they had: knives. And watching Julian sharpen them on an oilstone at the kitchen table gave them a false sense of security as they made their plans.

Paisley was going to direct them to the location, and Santo was going to pinpoint the spot. Nat was going to stay behind the wheel with the engine running, and Julian was going to stay near the car as a lookout. As soon as the burlap sacks were recovered, they would get the hell out of there. And after a quick detour to Six-thirteen to pick up the balance of their cargo, they would head for the Nextime Bar.

Once they arrived at the bar, their plans were . . . uncertain. Nat and Julian's positions would not change. And Santo would go in with Paisley to see Manford. From there on, it was anybody's guess.

Santo suddenly felt compelled to say something about the war . . . and how it might apply in this situation. But all that came out were mawkish-sounding words.

"You should always eat your last meal and smoke your last cigarette before going into combat."

Two of them chuckled apprehensively.

CHAPTER 23

Gladys

Sunset was in full bloom. And the sky was painted with bright amber colors accented by a long strip of white clouds.

Santo stretched. The horizon's beauty filled him with peace. He forgot about the tension, and the anger, and the crazy situation he was mixed up in, and began walking.

Shadows began to appear with the encroaching gray that preceded the sudden illumination of street lights; it was always a delicate time. Most people were either at home eating dinner during this hour or tucked away at a tavern in an attempt to soften the blow that had been their day.

When he reached the street corner, he saw a familiar figure approaching him on the sidewalk. It was Gladys.

"I couldn't sleep," she said. "So I laid on my mattress with wide open eyes. I couldn't avoid listening to the four of you."

"Then you know why I needed to take this walk and . . . you know as much as I do, Gladys."

They began walking together.

"I like you, Rick."

"You don't have to say that."

"No. But I do appreciate a real man, once in a while."

"Don't give me any more credit than I deserve. Truth is . . . I don't know what the hell I'm doing with my life."

"Well, you hide it better than the rest of us."

"Look. I'm just a burned-out vet who doesn't know how . . . or why . . . I survived the war. Sure, I'm back in the world. But all I've been trying to do is figure out what the hell happened to me there. That's all."

"I don't believe that."

"Why? Because we made love once?"

"Is that what you call it?" She smiled. "No. It's because you think your thoughts. You choose your words. You take action. Then . . . you don't look back."

"Shoot. That's all I do. Anyway . . . why are you telling me this?"

"I don't know." She broke her stride as if she was going to stop walking. But her stall was only a threat. "That's a lie. I need to talk with . . . well . . . someone like you."

"But . . . I'm nothing."

"You have the quality of truth."

He pursed his lips. "You're making me like you."

She peered into the sky. "It's a shame, isn't it?"

"What?"

"You and me . . . will probably never . . . really, make love."

"Does that really matter?"

She stuck an intimate hand into his nearest trouser pocket. "No. I guess not. But you've completed your final exam."

"Did I pass?"

"Well . . . you've got my trust."

"Why the sudden responsibility?"

"For the same reason you needed this walk."

"I needed to be alone."

"Then we have something in common."

They smiled at the contradiction and continued walking, immersed in a public privacy. And after awhile, she carefully interrupted their silence.

"What's it all about, Rick?"

He noticed the grays of twilight had changed into the shadows of dusk. "Look . . . the stars."

"Don't tease."

"I wouldn't do that."

She glanced at the stars. "Then . . . is that all there is?"

"I don't know. I . . . don't know anything."

"Neither do I." She sighed. "Everything has gotten so dull in my life. I'm bored." And after a thoughtful interval, "Will there be any meaning to my death?"

"I'm not sure that's the right question, Gladys."

"Then what is?"

"Will there be any meaning to my life?"

The impact of his answer washed evenly across her face. But her expression changed asymmetrically as if the mosaic pieces on one side of her portrait were crumbling.

"I like that," she said.

"I didn't say anything."

"Then, thank you for nothing."

She pulled her hand out of his pocket and linked her arm around his. Their brisk cadence changed to a stroll.

"Why a pimp in Atlanta?" he asked.

"I wonder how often that question has been asked."

"Just this once . . . between you and me."

"And that's all that counts. Is that the idea?"

"Something like that."

"Well," she said, "you'd be surprised how much money I can make. A lot of men are really turned on by the boyish look."

"Is that why you . . . shave between your . . . your . . ."

"It got your attention," she teased, "didn't it?"

"Yeah . . . well . . ."

"Look, hon, there was nothing wrong with what we did on the beach."

"Oh, for heaven's sake, I know that."

"Then stop blushing."

"Am I?"

Santo's vernal remark amused her.

"You're a strange one, Rick. You don't belong here."

"Where's that?"

"Beside me."

"You underestimate yourself."

"And at Six-thirteen."

"You also overestimate me."

"If I counted at all, I wouldn't be a prostitute."

"There you go again, labeling yourself."

And after wiping the surprised expression off her face, her features softened. "Stop being so wonderful."

He teased her. "It really is a shame, isn't it?"

"Yeah. It's really beginning to look that way."

Dusk had blossomed into evening with the circular flood of streetlights modifying the laws of nature. Their shadows disappeared and reappeared as they passed under the influence of each lamp.

"It's going to be dangerous," she said. "And I'm not sure it's worth it."

"It isn't."

"Then . . . why?"

"Because. The decision's been made."

"I don't think I'll ever understand that."

"I'm not sure you're supposed to."

"You mean, because I'm a woman?"

"No. Because you're a woman."

She tugged at his arm. "Come on. Tell me. I want to understand."

"But the odds are against you."

"Why?"

"Haven't you noticed? There are differences between a man and a woman."

"So what."

He stopped walking and studied her as she came around to face him.

"A decision like that reflects a man's discipline . . . and courage. Once he's committed . . . he can't . . . he shouldn't think anymore." He looked into her eyes. "You see? I failed." He started walking again. Gladys quickly caught up with him.

"What do you mean?"

"I've had to use words."

"Then shut up and hold my hand. Men." She shook her hair impetuously as if there had been a wind. "I'll probably never see you again once all this is over."

"I know. So, what's new?"

"Then you have no ties either."

"Look at me. What do you think?"

"You're welcome to come with me, Rick. I could support you, working in Atlanta."

"Thanks."

She understood the tone in his voice. "But, no thanks."

"It's not like that, Gladys."

She released his hand and stopped walking. "I know. I was being selfish." She bit her lower lip. "Melisa is really going to miss you."

"Her feelings don't run very deep. She'll get over it."

"You're right." Her disappointment was clear. "You see? I told you I was selfish."

"Women."

She threw a mischievous smile at him. "You're quick. And I'm not a very good actress."

"Come on. You had the right idea a minute ago."

"What?"

"Shut up and hold my hand."

They pushed aside the reality of their petty troubles and enjoyed the very presence of each other. It allowed the beauty of the night sky to confirm itself. Then Santo steered them back toward Six-thirteen. There was no need to wish upon a star.

CHAPTER 24

Almost Too Easy

Santo gently pressed the car's rear door shut until it clicked into place. The moon was high in the sky, making the hour too bright and the trees almost prehistoric.

Nat turned his head toward the noise of the car door closing and revealed a paranoid expression. Then he sank lower into his seat in response to the other doors opening and closing: first Julian, then Paisley, who also blinded him with the flash of the interior light. All that could be seen of Nat was his cowboy hat.

"Sit tight, Nat."

"Easy for you to say."

Santo scanned the area until his taut lips dissolved. Then he raised his arm and pointed at a familiar area. "Over there."

He and Paisley moved into the thick shadows among the trees, leaving Nat and Julian exposed on the open field. Then Santo stopped, looked around to get a fix on his position, and began running in an effort to reconstruct last night's perceptions. Paisley was startled by his sudden departure but quickly perceived what he was attempting to do. He caught up with him, then stayed close behind.

Familiarity came with the frantic zigzagging around trees. It seemed to set off a radar, which led Santo to the spot he was looking for. He approached the base of the knoll and started clearing away the leaves. Paisley couldn't help asking the obvious question.

"Is that the place?"

It would have been easy to be sarcastic but Santo resisted the temptation. He raised one of the burlap sacks into view, instead.

"Wonderful." Paisley snatched it from his hand. "You saved my ass, you know that, don't you?"

"The night's not over, compadre. Let's get the hell out of here. Nat should be ready to have a baby by now."

Paisley chuckled.

They ran back to the car, jumped in, and listened to their hearts pounding as Nat drove away from the fairgrounds. Julian released a primal scream as soon as the car hit the safety of the pavement.

"Goddamn it! We did it. We did it!"

The pressure had been too intense not to respond to his emotional release.

"Yeeehaaa!" Nat cried as the vehicle rocked with the shouting and the tremors of four men.

"This was almost too easy," Julian declared.

"You said that the last time. Look where it got us."

Julian's expression flattened.

"Come on, Rick. Don't kill the party," Nat said.

"When the man's right, he's right," Julian said. "We've still got a long night ahead of us."

The satisfaction of their achievement gradually faded and gave way to the tension of cigarette smoke. The uncertainty of their future made them inhale deeply and hold the smoke in their lungs longer than usual before releasing the gray vapor into the humid atmosphere.

They were going through the motions and were men enough to know it.

CHAPTER 25

The Madness and Confusion of Battle

Rick's hands shook from hunger as he tore open his long-rats of beef and rice. He poured water from his canteen into the plastic pouch and stirred the concoction with a white plastic spoon. The food smelled good.

Other than smoking, food was the only pleasure available to them in the bush. He tried not to eat too fast while he watched Russo studying his map in search of a good LZ.

After awhile, Russo approached him with the map and sat down on a clump of weeds beside him. Rick took another bite of his food before peering into Russo's stony face.

"Half a click to the southwest is a good LZ." Russo shoved the map over to him, pointing to the area. "What do you think?"

He scanned it carefully. "Looks good to me."

"Then finish your chow. We're moving out soon." Russo stood up. "I don't know; something doesn't feel right. It's beginning to make me nervous." Then he went to Wishbone to make radio contact with headquarters to establish a rendezvous.

Rick hoped he would be as good a patrol leader as Russo when they finally offered him that position. He wolfed down the rest of his chow.

They traveled to their destination at a snail's pace, cursing the terrain that fought them every step of the way. And when they neared the rendezvous point, the sound of the choppers forced them into a furious gallop that left them exhausted at the edge of the LZ.

Suddenly, the choppers were in sight: two Hueys, one Cobra, and a Forty-Six. Rick listened to Russo making radio contact and waited for his signal to pop the green smoke. Russo nodded.

He released the smoke and tossed the canister in the direction where the wind would carry the smoke away from them. Then they walked into the clearing with the green smoke to their backs and watched the choppers descend upon them like locusts.

A puff of white smoke spewed from one of the Hueys as it fired one of its rockets. The explosion that followed made them crouch to the ground. Then the other gunships also began destroying everything around them.

Suddenly, Rick heard Russo shouting. "Pop the red smoke! Pop the red smoke!"

Bearcat quickly reacted. The red smoke engulfed them, and the Forty-Six Sea Knight veered into their direction.

"Charlie's here," Russo shouted.

"How do you know?" Rick asked.

"Because the choppers got a bunch of green smokes from Charlie."

Rick clenched his teeth and directed his gaze at the tree line surrounding them. Then he clicked the safety off his rifle, knowing this was it. He went blank and threw away his life in order to stalk the present. Then his mind filled up with a reverse image of himself seen at an angle from above. He crouched in the heat of the tall elephant grass, with his face looking skyward, like an artificial flower taunting life with an attitude of permanence.

The Forty-Six's approach brought a circular wind of dirt and sand and smoke that temporarily blinded them and pressed the surrounding elephant grass to the ground. It hovered tentatively near them before it landed. Then a stream of rapid fire cut through the ground between Happy and Kafka, separating them with a line of dust. They'd made enemy contact.

The team responded with a flurry of haphazard gunfire while the M-60's on the Forty-Six began firing in support. The enemy appeared: figures to the left, figures to the right, figures all around cutting through the tall grass.

Rick aimed his rifle at a small group and brought two of them down. Then he heard himself scream like a madman as he charged at them in a blind rage. He saw Bearcat blast a man to a bloody pulp and saw Happy beating one to death with the butt of his rifle. The madness and confusion of battle took over as they fought desperately to keep the Viet Cong away from the aircraft. But when he heard a couple of RPG's explode near the chopper, he almost panicked: even an indirect hit could blow an aircraft to hell.

"Make it for the chopper! Make it for the chopper!"

They quickly retreated. They knew it wouldn't be able to wait for them much longer.

Rick took one last aim and brought another figure down to his knees in agony. Then he turned toward the chopper and started running. He saw Kafka fall, screaming for the corpsman they didn't have. But Bearcat scooped him up as if he was a rag doll and threw him over his shoulder, hardly breaking his stride.

The aircraft sat thirty meters away with its rear gate open like a steel mouth and with its side gunners spitting small bits of death at the enemy. From their angle of approach, Rick could see the pilot sitting calmly in his cockpit waiting for them. His windows were riddled with bullet holes, and the sounds of metal and confused men were everywhere.

Rick saw Sunny take a hit. Its impact spun him off his feet, and the weight of his backpack made him land on his back. Rick passed his rifle off to Mormon as he steered in Sunny's direction. And when he reached him, Sunny was holding his right thigh with both hands.

"It's my leg, man, it's my fucking leg!"

Rick grabbed Sunny's rifle and assisted him onto his good leg. They hung onto each other and hobbled toward the aircraft like a broken land crab, certain that they weren't going to make it.

Rick heard Russo shouting at them from the chopper to hurry up. And just when his strength was about to fail him, Rick felt several strong hands assist him and Sunny the rest of the way. It was Russo and Bearcat.

The four of them slipped on the deck as they entered the chopper and tumbled in all directions. Rick managed to stand up but slipped again on the blood. Then he noticed Happy lying unconscious and unattended in a heap against the bulkhead.

Rick couldn't understand why the chopper hadn't taken off yet. And when he saw the others shooting out the windows, he grabbed a stray rifle to assist them. Then Rick heard a loud ping.

He staggered, saw black, and fell.

A pink tornado engulfed Rick and drained him of his energy. Then the tornado disengaged from Rick and moved several feet away from him before the narrow lower part of the whirlwind leaped into the air. The tornado shifted sideways until it was parallel to the ground, and the wide upper part of the whirlwind was facing Rick.

There was a forest-pond nestled on the top of the tornado. Rick felt drawn to this glassy surface as would a butterfly. But explosions and excited voices disturbed the calm.

A wary figure emerged from the pond's clouded depth and stood over him. It was Mormon. "Rick! Rick, are you hit? Rick! Are you hit?"

Rick thought he heard Mormon say he was hit. And in a panic, he reached for his forehead.

"Oh my God!" he cried, as he felt blood oozing from a lump. The chopper finally lifted for the sky.

He stood up in a panic and heard Mormon laughing. Rick felt the lump on his head again and realized the wound wasn't serious.

"Must have been a ricochet off that window!" Mormon yelled as he continued to laugh. "You were lucky!"

Rick blinked his eyes nervously and pressed both hands against his forehead to confirm that statement about his luck.

CHAPTER 26

It's Too Late

Kerry and the women refused to show any relief over the successful recovery of the burlap sacks. They knew the real danger was still ahead. And when the car pulled away from the curb, the three of them stood on the sidewalk in front of Six-thirteen, frozen into a composition of helplessness.

When they arrived at the Nextime Bar, Santo noticed two unsavory characters loitering in the rear parking lot. The gesture between them revealed that they recognized Nat's vehicle. Then they melted into the blue shadows.

"That was no coincidence," Santo said. "I don't like this already, Paisley."

"It's too late to do anything about it now."

"Then if we're going to go, let's go in style," Julian said, as he brandished a sharp kitchen knife.

"Put that stupid thing away," Paisley said. "All you're going to do with that is piss them off."

"Who says?"

"What are you getting at, Julian?" Santo said.

"A change in plans. I'm not going to stay out here like a sitting duck. And you shouldn't either, Nat."

"Okay," Nat said, as he pulled his keys out of the ignition. "But I kind of agree with Pais. I don't think these knives are going to be much good against these people."

"You're probably right. But I say we at least call their bluff or . . . or . . . at least show them that we're not afraid. Something. Anything to give us an edge to cut them with. You don't scare these kind of people, man, unless you make them bleed a little." Julian looked at Paisley. "I'm going to help you out just this once. But so help me, I'll break your face if you ever get me into something like this again . . . in Atlanta or any other place we might end up together after this."

"Look," Nat interrupted. "There's two more prowling over there at the entrance of the parking lot."

"Shit."

"I promise you, Julian. I swear," Paisley said.

Julian threw a mean glance at him. "I hear you."

"Well then . . . each of you grab a sack," Santo said. "Let's go."

They all got out of the car, intimidating the two guys standing in the shadows of the building. They melted away in response to the small band's approach: one through the rear door of the bar and the other around the side of the building. The other two maintained their distance near the entrance of the parking lot. Santo took charge.

"Stay in pairs. Julian, Nat, follow that other guy around front and come in through the main entrance. Paisley and I will take the back door. Here, let me have those sacks." He ended up with three of the burlap sacks while Paisley carried the fourth, along with the box of cocaine. "Okay. This is it. You two work your way through the bar into the pool hall. Manford's office is in the rear left corner of the place. If you hear any trouble . . . well . . . this is not everyone for themselves this time."

"Can I count on you guys?"

"We're here, ain't we?" Nat said.

Santo stepped between him and Paisley. "Save it for those guys inside, Nat."

The two pairs broke off in opposite directions.

Santo and Paisley paused near the back door for a few moments to give Nat and Julian time to enter the bar. Then Santo opened the rear door and invited Paisley to enter first.

The pool hall was more crowded than the night before last, and the sound of billiards balls banged and banked off the tables more frequently. The office door was open, and the light was on. Manford appeared at the door's threshold with a sinister smile streaked horizontally across his face. He motioned them to hurry as he stood there waiting to shut the door behind him. Santo was surprised to find Manford alone.

"I see you have the merchandise."

"Yeah, Mr. Manford," Paisley said.

Under Manford's intense scrutiny, Santo set the three burlap sacks he was carrying on the desk. Then Manford glanced at the box Paisley was carrying, ignoring the fourth sack.

"Well?"

"Well, what?" Paisley said.

"Let's have a look."

Paisley approached the desk while Santo shifted to a position near the door. Then Manford opened and tested the cocaine. He appeared to be pleased.

"I don't suppose you'll be able to appreciate this," he said, with his eyes firmly planted on the cocaine. "But you were part of an experiment. I'm sure you've noted a few irregularities."

Paisley shifted uneasily. "Yeah. So?"

"So, doesn't that make you a little curious?"

"Just pay me what you owe me and I'll disappear."

"I'm curious," Santo said.

"Good." Manford actually smiled. "First of all, Paisley was supposed to work alone. He didn't. Secondly, he was never expected to return. As a decoy, he was supposed to be caught. His escape placed the real shipment in jeopardy. The cops were swarming all over North Florida last night. And finally, for reasons that will always remain a secret, this is a one-way trip for you, Paisley." Manford pulled out a revolver from his desk drawer. It had a large silencer attached to the end of the muzzle. "But now, it's a one-way trip for both of you."

"You son of a bitch," Paisley said. Manford pointed the threatening revolver at him. "What are you slimeballs up to?"

"You're the slimeball. And you're up to dying. That's all you have to know," he said coldly.

Santo quickly reached for the light switch by the door and pushed it down. The sudden darkness produced several concentrated flashes from the silencer. Santo crouched low against the wall in response.

"You motherfucker!" Paisley cried.

Manford fired the revolver two more times before Santo heard Paisley lock onto Manford in a struggle. And when he switched on the lights to render Paisley assistance, he saw him bury his knife deep into Manford's chest. Manford gasped, dropped the revolver, and fell heavily to the floor. Then Paisley staggered against the desk for support before he slumped down onto his rump beside him. The front of his shirt was crimson with blood.

Santo ran over to him. "Paisley!"

"The son of a bitch got me on the third shot."

Santo found the telephone and lifted it off the receiver. "We've got to get you to the hospital."

"I don't feel good, man."

"No shit, you idiot." He started dialing. "You'll be alright. Jail is better than being dead, right?" But there was no answer.

He hung up the telephone and approached Paisley to assess his condition. There was no breath, no pulse, no life.

Manford was also dead. He searched through his pockets and discovered about five hundred dollars in cash.

"Sorry about this, Pais. But we need this money to get out of town. Take care, buddy."

He turned off the lights and slipped out of the office. He didn't understand why nobody heard the scuffle or the muffled shots.

He walked to the nearest unoccupied billiards table and scanned the pool hall for Julian and Nat. Then the realization of what had just happened smashed through his brain and paralyzed him; he leaned against the table for support.

Death had been no stranger to him, but this was different. This was a criminal affair that could ruin the rest of his life. He wasn't prepared to allow that to happen. Not after surviving a tour of duty in Vietnam.

Careful voices approached him as he regained his composure.

"Rick, baby, are you alright?" Julian said.

"Yeah, man. I'm okay."

Nat placed a heavy hand on his shoulder. "Are you sure?"

"Yeah, yeah."

"Where's Paisley?"

Santo had enough sense to whisper. "He's dead."

"He's what? Holy shit."

"We've got to get the hell out of here," Julian hissed.

"You've got that right," Santo said.

"What the hell is all this about?"

"Who the hell knows. But as long as we're here, Nat, we're bait. Come on. Some of the players are beginning to look at us. I think the front entrance is probably the safest way out."

"But my car."

"It's no good if you're dead."

"We're dead without it."

"Nat's right."

"Okay, okay, let's go."

They left the bar through the back door and went straight for the car. The parking lot was deserted.

"What the hell is going on around here?"

"Shit. This is creepy."

"Right on."

They piled into the Chevrolet.

"Never again. Never."

Nat started the car and drove out of the parking lot.

CHAPTER 27

"Welcome home, soldier."

It was dark. And they looked like three ghosts sitting in the front seat of a parked car at Southgate Apartments. They were almost afraid to move.

"Crazy."

"You think they followed us?"

"Dead."

"I didn't see any lights on in the house."

"Stupid."

"I think we're safe."

They sought confirmation from the following silence.

"I think you're right, Rick," Nat finally said. "What do you think, Julian?"

"What?"

"You think my car is hot?"

"How should I know? But if it isn't, it's a miracle."

"That's for sure," Santo said.

"What the hell happened in there, man?"

"This guy, Manford, pulled a gun on us. I flicked off the lights, and Paisley went for him. A few shots later, I turned on the lights and saw Paisley bury his knife into Manford's chest. Paisley was badly shot and died before I could do anything for him."

"And Manford?"

"He's dead, too."

"Jesus Christ," Nat muttered.

"I don't get none of this," Julian said. "They let us go. Why?"

"I don't know."

A slow and bewildered whistle escaped from Julian in response. "Man."

"This is too much for me," Nat said. "Hey, I'm just an ordinary guy."

"What happened to the four bags of weed and—"

"I left it all behind, Julian."

"But . . . but that was a lot of stuff, man."

"Yeah. And maybe . . . just maybe . . . they'll really leave us alone."

"Maybe. And maybe—"

"Just maybe, he's right," Nat interjected, with a finality that led to a silence as dark as the unlit parking lot surrounding them.

They stared straight ahead like three ceramic owls until a tap on the rear window startled them. Julian hit his right knee against the window crank.

"Jesus Christ!"

"Shit!"

"Hey guys," Kerry said.

"Goddamn it! Scare the hell out of us, why don't you."

"Sorry, Richard. I saw you all drive by. Is anything wrong? Where's Paisley?"

"What happened to the lights?" Santo asked, avoiding Kerry's question.

"What lights?" Julian said.

"I noticed they were out when we drove by."

"The electricity has been cut off," Kerry said.

"How come?"

"Looks like somebody didn't pay the utilities."

"Are you sure it's the utilities?"

"We're the only dark house on the street and the fuses in the box aren't blown."

"Well," Santo said, "that's why they invented candles, right?"

"If you say so," Kerry said. "Where's Paisley?"

Santo waited until they were safely in Six-thirteen's porch before answering Kerry's question. "He's dead."

The light of a match shattered the darkness before touching a candle wick.

"Who's dead?" Gladys asked in a tremulous voice before blowing out the match.

"I'm sorry, Gladys . . . Paisley."

The flame danced and curled in response to a draft. She sat down, looking stunned. "Are we safe?"

"I don't know, Gladys. I'm not sure about anything anymore," he said.

"What happened?"

Santo explained the details once again. But he left out most of his vocal inflection because he was tired. He stripped the story to the bone; it left them feeling cold.

"We've run out of luck," she concluded. "I need a drink. Do we have anything left?"

"There's wine in the refrigerator," Melisa said.

Santo escorted her into the kitchen. The edge of the counter guided them to the refrigerator where he found what she was looking for. She drank deeply and with the need to alter her state of mind.

"Can I do anything for you?" he asked.

"Don't worry, hon, I'm fine."

His eyes had grown accustomed to the dark; he could see Melisa approaching them.

"Is there anything I can do, Gladys?" Melisa said.

"I'd like to get some fresh air."

"Come on, hon. I'll take her, Rick."

"Be careful, okay?"

"Don't worry, I've got her."

He sat down at the kitchen table with the bottle of wine as they dissolved into the darkness.

"Take care of her, Melisa," Julian said, as he emerged from the darkness. He found a chair and sat on the opposite side of the table. "I can sure use a hit off that wine."

He pushed the bottle toward Julian and watched him drink voraciously. When Julian was finished, he set the empty bottle on the table.

"That's how it used to happen in country," Julian murmured. "Suddenly . . . there was death."

"Yeah. In country. You've been to Nam."

"Army. You?"

"Marine Corps."

"Yeah," Julian said. "Sometimes they just wouldn't be around anymore. Like Paisley. I don't know which was worse: to see them get wasted, or feel their nonexistence."

"What outfit were you with?"

"187th Infantry Battalion. Alpha Company."

"Then you saw action."

"Yeah. And you?"

"First Recon. 1st Marine Division."

Julian acknowledged the unit's combat reputation. "Welcome home, soldier."

"Yeah. Welcome home."

CHAPTER 28

If It Hadn't Been for the Dying . . .

The morning brought sunlight and cold showers in the wake of their power cut-off. It was a new day. And they were safe. Thoughts of Paisley were already pressed into the past.

A cup of coffee cooked on a Sterno can, which Gladys bought that morning at a nearby convenience store, was placed into Santo's hand. He was grateful for Melisa's attentiveness, but he realized he was growing weary of this scene.

He couldn't continue living off the land like this; he was beginning to lose his self-respect. He couldn't place his finger on the problem, but he knew he had to get away. He looked at Six-thirteen's surroundings: the mistreated furniture, the neglected house, the general abuse, the plain vandalism. He experienced a deeper loss of pride after identifying these conditions and decided he had to address this problem sometime in the near future. Because his future, or the lack of one, was at the core of his dissatisfaction.

It was late in the morning before he decided to shake himself loose from a sofa on the front porch. He found out Gladys and Melisa had gone shopping for more beer, wine, cigarettes, coffee, candles, and a Coleman cooking stove. Nat drove them.

Gladys was crazy for bouncing checks the way she did. It was only a matter of time before she ended up in jail.

He forced himself out of the house and into the sun and found himself wandering on campus before he regained full consciousness.

The day was beautiful. The trees were green. The faces of the students were bright. He liked the campus's fresh feeling, and he envied the students' sense of life, direction, and purpose . . . all the things, in fact, that he lacked in his own life. He reached deep within himself and touched his scar: the war, the pain, the faces of the dead. It would have been easy to blame Vietnam for everything: his emptiness, his shiftlessness, his confusion, his loneliness of not belonging and . . . and his guilt of surviving. He had killed and had been killed. He stood in this wake of death feeling dull and arid and uncreated. But he was unable to plunge into misery.

He observed himself from a place outside of himself as he walked. This experience finally startled him. He remembered when this first happened in Vietnam. And now, with the absence of combat-fear. He blinked his eyes and shook his head and did not force himself to understand.

Santo quickened his pace and wondered, what was he doing?

He had everything to be thankful for: he made it back from the war in one piece; he was back in his world almost as if he'd never left.

Almost. Yes. That was the word that kept him separated, that stood between him and his world. It was almost that kept the war alive within him . . . all the time . . . every day. And it made him feel like a stranger. He almost wanted to go back.

He missed its intensity. The men. The comradeship. The brotherhood. If it hadn't been for the dying . . .

He listened to the laughter of men at one moment and to their tears in the next. Then he wondered if he was going insane—his anxiety peaked: to cry, without a cry . . . tears.

The sound of country music in a passing car brought him back into the present and prevented him from stepping off the sidewalk into a busy street. The blare of a horn shattered his silent turmoil and intensified his alienation. He felt a firm hand on his shoulder.

"Hey, man, are you alright?"

The concerned expression in Julian's large, primitive-looking features could have been sculpted by Picasso.

"I think so."

Another voice came from his left and disoriented him, again.

"Are you sure?"

"Kerry."

He placed a supportive arm around Santo. "We were in the neighborhood, honey."

"Were you guys following me?"

"Now why would we do a thing like that to a friend . . . and a manic-depressive."

"Hey, man, watch what you say."

"He might be right, Julian."

"Bullshit, man. It's the war. I travel the same road myself, remember?"

"Oh . . . yeah," Santo distantly acknowledged.

"Don't let him fall, Kerry!"

"I've got him!"

"I'm alright."

Julian was supporting him as well. "Sure you are."

"Julian?"

"Yeah?"

"How long has it been for you?"

"I've been back a year . . . plus a lifetime."

"Does it ever go away?"

"I don't know, my man. It does get better. But I don't think, no, never . . . never away."

"I'll take better."

"Don't worry, you'll get it . . . in time . . . I hope. Hell, I don't know. Look at me. I haven't got much better. What do I know? You got any money?"

"A little."

"How about a beer?"

"Where?"

"There's a little bar next to the Co-op Bookstore," Kerry said.

"That's too close to the Nextime, man."

"No, it isn't," Kerry insisted. "They're half a street away from each other, and they have a completely different kind of clientele."

"It better not be a gay bar."

"They're worlds apart, that's all."

"What do you think, Rick?" Julian asked.

"What the hell. Let's go."

"Alright. I ain't worried if you're not."

They had three quick beers apiece. And when they left the bar, they were assaulted by a painfully bright sun. It forced them to take a detour into the Co-op Bookstore.

The wooden floors creaked under the weight of their footsteps as they invaded the two rooms of shelved new and used books and magazine racks full of leftist underground periodicals. A hairy-headed guy, absorbed in a book, sat behind the counter. He looked up, smiled, and didn't ask if they needed any help.

Julian wanted to leave. But Santo liked the musty smell of the place and, most of all, its quiet serenity. They stayed.

Kerry remained with the periodicals, leafing through gay activist literature; Julian discovered, to his satisfaction, a section on black history and literature; and Santo wandered into the next room, where he discovered philosophy and drama.

Santo was unfamiliar with most of the authors on the shelves. But he was fascinated by them. He recognized important names and felt their mystery: Gogol, Singer, Forster, Rand, Kafka, Shakespeare, Bashô, Sartre, Hilton, Woolrich, Doyle, Brontë, Horace, Gibbon, Kazantzakis, Paine, Marx, Aristotle, Plato, Saint Augustine,

Stanislavski, O'Neill, Ibsen, Williams, Chekhov, Hesse, Hemingway . . . names, names he only heard of . . . names that were familiar . . . and kindly reminded him of his ignorance. There was so much to do in this life. He'd seen nothing, yet. He knew nothing!

That was no way to die . . . or live.

He suddenly felt intimidated by the height of the books surrounding him and lost his equilibrium. He stumbled backwards and almost fell. But he regained his balance with an intricate maneuver, dropping the paperback book he had in his hand. It hit the floor flat and unharmed: *A Moon for the Misbegotten*.

He picked up the book and reshelved it. He felt despair and didn't know why. Then he raised his head and looked into the tormented blue eyes of a red-bearded face. It was a glossy print of Vincent Van Gogh . . . a self-portrait. And as he stood before him, he could see the genius of his work and the intensity of his universe. He was shouting at the world with his colors and didn't understand why people couldn't see. But Santo saw. He could see!

He was startled away from his reverie.

"Hey, man, what's up?"

He responded to Julian's restlessness by walking out of the bookstore into the blinding sun, feeling a bit mad.

They followed him across Tennessee Street and engaged themselves in the spirit of his purposelessness while they accompanied him into the older side of the campus. It was a disjointed segment of his psyche that carried them through an undetermined period of time, which came to a conclusion when Santo realized they were sitting in the last row of a darkened theatre. He couldn't remember how they got there.

The actors on stage stood under harsh working lights. And their distant voices projected intense emotion. Then an authoritative voice from the fifth row of the house interrupted them. The figure stood up.

The actors responded so positively to the man's directions that Santo became captivated by their trust . . . by their concentration . . . by their make-believe world. He slid into a lower, more comfortable, position and listened to the director.

"Take it from the top. 'Why are you always in black?' "

They ran through the scene again.

"Good . . . but, Masha, I want you to skip around the bench when you enter this time."

She looked confused. "Skip? But . . ."

"Do it," the director said. Then he decided to clarify some of her doubts. "Look, Masha, it's not that great a play. It's a play. That's all. You walk and you talk. Just say the words. Forget about all the things you've read and heard."

"But . . . this is Chekhov," she said meekly.

The director climbed onto the stage. "And he's dead. Let's not kill the poor bastard again with monotony." He threw up his hands. "Look . . . people . . . what do you think I've been trying to do with you? I don't want you the same! You're flesh and blood! That means you don't agree on the same concepts. Maybe she wears black because she's not intelligent enough to do anything else. It doesn't matter! Let me worry about the through-line of the show. All you've got to do is be . . . and become people with all their variations. You don't have to agree with each other's motives. My God, you don't even have to agree on the play's theme. And don't ask me what it is because I'm not going to tell you. Just let me worry about the unity and the rhythm of this production. You . . . you worry about yourselves. Stop agreeing! The only time you should be listening to each other is when you're on stage. Stop intellectualizing. Again! 'Why are you always in black?' "

The director jumped off the stage into the darkness.

The scene started and stopped several more times with the director growing more satisfied. It amazed Santo how calmly the man shouted, making the actors feel as if it was for their own good. He had a talent for clarifying and orchestrating and inspiring confident performances on stage.

"This must be a theatre practice," Julian whispered.

"It's a rehearsal," Kerry said.

The director stood up and spoke vehemently at the actors on stage.

"Medvedenko, if you don't stop acting I'm going to turn the house lights back on! Masha, shorten the word 'performance.' It's not necessary to pour everything you believe in about the play into one word. Besides, it's impossible to do. You can't assume the audience knows anything. If they don't see it, it doesn't exist. Understand? 'It won't be long before the performance.' That's all there is to say. Let the playwright do the work. Again. Places."

The characters started again.

Santo was fascinated by the director's attention to emotional detail: each one specific to the needs of the actor and the moment. It seemed as if it didn't matter what the actors thought or how they worked to get there. But the effect . . . the transformation into life was astounding.

"Good, Masha. Medvedenko, late on, 'I don't want any.' And pause for only one beat following him, Masha. 'I don't want any.' Beat. 'It's stifling.' Good. Both of you. Do you understand where we're going? Good. From the top. And I won't interrupt you this time. Good. When you're ready."

The director's energy was electric. He lit a cigarette, pleased by the progress.

When you're ready, Santo echoed internally, as he began to feel the familiar tension of an ambush firing lane. *Ready on the right,* he heard. *Ready on the left.*

Santo sank lower into his chair as he broke into a cold sweat and his peripheral vision suddenly narrowed. The darkened distance from the last row of the theatre to the lighted stage became equal to the distance from the firing line to the kill zone.

He saw the actors on stage, then he heard a branch breaking in the bush; he saw human shadows, then he heard explosions and the cry of men. No separation.

Santo strained against his chair as his past merged with the present. What was happening to him? What—

"Hey, man, are you alright?" Julian asked.

Kerry placed the palm of his hand against Santo's chest. "He's shivering. Damn, is he having a flashback?"

"Hell, I . . . I don't know." Julian nudged Santo with his elbow. "Hey, man, that play-acting up there looks too much like work."

Santo brushed Kerry's hand from his chest, then caressed himself by crossing his right arm over his left.

Julian broke into Santo's attentive shell with another disrupting whisper.

"Hey, man, what's up?"

Disappointed, Santo knew it was time to leave. But not without realizing that he just experienced something special, something alien to most of the world. He didn't attempt to label the experience. They eased out of the theatre into the lobby.

"What is this place?" Santo asked.

"It's the Conradi Theatre," Kerry said. "It's a neat little place, isn't it?"

"Yeah."

"Come on, let's go down to the student union and see what's going on," Julian said restlessly.

But they went back to Six-thirteen, instead, and found Melisa cooking in the kitchen on a Coleman stove. She was stirring something in a pot.

"Where's Nat and Gladys?" Julian asked.

"Asleep," she said, indicating Gladys's and Paisley's old room with her eyes. Then she misinterpreted Santo's expression. "A girl's got to make a living."

"Go, Nat-man," Julian said. He nudged Santo. "Life waits for nobody, right?"

Kerry stuck his inquisitive nose near the edge of the pot. "What have you got in here, dearie?"

She directed her answer to Santo. "Just an old-fashioned stew."

"It smells good," Santo said.

"It sure does," Kerry said.

"It's an easy one-pot dish to cook."

"Very nice," Kerry said supportively. "And very domestic, don't you think, Richard?"

Santo understood Melisa's motive. But he was unsure about Kerry's. Was he being sincere, or did he detect a hint of maliciousness in Kerry's voice?

Maybe Kerry was trying to push their relationship into a confrontation. But then what? Kerry couldn't be seriously hoping to develop a relationship with him.

"Yeah. Very domestic," Santo said.

Julian went to the refrigerator before realizing that it was no longer running. But his shattered hope for a cold beer was salvaged when he discovered a Styrofoam ice chest full of beer on the floor beside it. Julian opened two cans and handed him one.

Santo left the kitchen by going through the rear door into Six-thirteen's back yard for the first time. It was a scruffy area full of ruts and weeds and barren spots, reflecting considerable neglect.

The droppings from the yard's only tree littered the area with leaves and twigs and bark, all in various stages of decay.

The sun was distressfully bright and intensified his discomfort with himself. He brought the can of beer to his lips and drank it to the bottom, hoping for a momentary rush of well-being; there wasn't any.

"There's no use beating yourself to death," Julian said. Then he laughed. "Women."

"I don't want to talk, Julian."

"Then listen. Because I've got to talk. I've had to talk since I've been back. But all I've done is . . . is scream into the night with my dreams. That's why I try to stay high all the time, I guess."

"Does it work?"

"Are you kidding?"

"I didn't do anything wrong in the war, Julian. I've killed . . . and I've been killed. But I didn't murder anybody over there. I didn't do anything I couldn't live with when I got back."

"Maybe that's my problem." Julian finished the rest of his beer. "I forgot I was coming home. You know what I mean?"

"Yeah. If you say so."

"I do." He brought the can of beer to his mouth, forgetting he'd finished it. Irritably, he tossed the can into the yard. "It was so hard to remember what it was like back in the world . . . the world. Here we are . . . and look at it." Julian peered into the sky in an effort to sanctify himself. "I did terrible things over there, man. I forgot I was a good person. I was scared and mad, and I did terrible things because I forgot." It appeared as if he was reenacting something. "Then I lived. How was I supposed to know I was going to live? I . . . cut off ears. I . . . counted teeth and confirmed kills. I . . . saw so many friends die that it made me kill in anger. I even wielded revenge against the innocent. What am I going to do, Rick?"

"I don't know, man. I really don't know." A brief moment passed between them. "Do you think there's a right and a wrong?"

Julian nodded. "Yeah. Like black and white."

"Then . . . forgive yourself."

"I'm trying man. I'm trying." Then he took a newspaper from under his arm and unfolded it in an attempt to change the painful subject. "They're calling Paisley's death a gangland murder."

Santo looked at the paper without reading it. "Then I guess we're off the hook."

"I guess."

"There's good and bad in everything. Don't try to figure it out, man."

"I'm not. I can't."

"Paisley's dead, and life is short, and . . . the war is over for you and me."

Santo didn't know if he really believed in what he just said about the war. But he repeated it to himself anyway.

He'd seen the dead. He'd been dead. He'd eaten his last meal and smoked his last cigarette prepared to be dead.

He looked into the bright sky and felt the mortality of it all. But he also felt the need to make his life count even if nothing mattered anyway . . . anyway . . . anyway . . .

CHAPTER 29

The South China Sea

The chopper changed course and threw Rick off balance. He crashed against a bulkhead and fell on top of Happy, who was wounded in the chest. He peered aft, in a daze, and noted the carnage:

One of the side gunners was wasted. He was slumped across his M-60 with his aviation helmet torn off and his forehead missing. Sunny was resisting Russo's help by holding onto his leg with both hands in an effort to stop the pain. And Kafka was crying as Bearcat attended to his gut wound.

Mormon pushed him aside to assist Happy. He knew Rick was still a bit stunned by the blow to his head.

Rick felt the wind blowing violently around him as he stood up. He staggered and danced over the discarded web gear in a vain attempt to gain a foothold. He tripped on a cartridge belt instead.

"Easy does it!" Wishbone shouted, above the noise of the chopper. He was sitting calmly against a bulkhead with his backpack and radio still strapped to his back. He lit two cigarettes and gave Rick one. "Come on, have a seat and stay out of their way! They've got enough to do without having to worry about you!"

Rick gratefully inhaled the sweet-tasting smoke, then managed to stand up. "Thanks!"

He noted the other side gunner standing by his partner and, instead of sitting down, he assisted him with the dead man; they laid him near the cockpit's entrance and covered his face with a blanket.

"He was a new guy!" the gunner shouted. "Just got in country!"

"That's a tough break!" Rick passed him his cigarette.

"That's the way it always seems to work! They either get it in the beginning or just before they're going home! It doesn't make any sense!"

"No, it doesn't!"

Rick looked through the window and saw the cobalt blue South China Sea below them. The gunner handed the cigarette back to him and poked his head into the cockpit. Rick inhaled another drag and noted the rare beauty of the water. Then he tapped the gunner on the shoulder to get his attention. "Hey! Where are we going?"

The gunner looked over his shoulder and shouted, "Hospital Ship!"

Bearcat was already pointing at the white ship with the red cross on its side to the others by the time Rick turned to them with the news. The wounded were either calm or unconscious; their battle dressings were soaked with blood.

The chopper hit the flight deck hard. And when the rear gate was lowered, Rick helped Mormon carry Happy out onto the flight deck where they were met by a horde of white coats and clean faces. They quickly snatched Happy away, leaving them feeling empty and self-conscious in a place where everything looked crystal clean and clear. They felt like aliens standing on the face of the moon, like strangers in a strange land.

The remaining wounded and the dead gunner were also carried away, leaving the others in a state of shock. They backed into the aircraft like demented spirits, overwhelmed by the experience. The chopper lifted to the sky.

The wind blew.

The chopper whirred loudly.

There were three brothers, gone forever.

CHAPTER 30

Impotence

The world was safe, again. Candles twinkled everywhere in Six-thirteen, giving each room a comforting aura of light.

Santo thought he heard wind chimes. But they were too clear and steady for this to be the wind. He followed the sound to the front porch and found Melisa standing in a corner nudging, with her finger, a menagerie of brass butterflies hanging on strings.

"I found these on the floor behind the chair." She pointed to the ceiling. "See the hook? The string must have broken." She seemed mesmerized by their metallic sound and their dancing shadows on the wall. "Don't you ever get tired of being alone, Rick?"

He knew she was reaching for the help he couldn't give her. So he revealed his emotional impotence.

"I can't help you, Melisa."

She ignored his answer. "It's raining."

He went to the screen door and looked out into the wetness. The street lights glared off the oily sheen on the wet road. Then he shifted to one side to make room for her. But she walked past him, through the door, and into the rain before she stopped.

"Where are you going?" he asked. She didn't answer. "What are you doing?"

The rain grew heavier. It began to plaster Melisa's hair against her head and down the sides of her face.

He went to her. She kissed him.

"Come with me," she said.

They began to walk in the rain like a pair of lost souls. The streets were slick and barren, the pat of rain against their faces a respite from the humidity.

They heard music in the distance. It sounded as if wind chimes had been laced into the notes. Then they saw movement in the light of a window. Its incandescence attracted them like a pair of moths.

The light rhythm of a drum and the melodic contrivance of an electric guitar encouraged them to step closer and closer until they reached the front door. They peered inside.

They were completely wet. But they were cleansed. Then they melted into each other's arms and froze into a soddened statue.

Individual musicians joined in or broke away from the music's continuous but ever-changing through-line whenever they wanted to. Consequently, the music's dynamics remained fresh and alluring and spontaneous. They balanced form with formlessness without being empty.

Santo felt liberated from time. There was nothing more than the concrete reality of this instant. The past and the future were abstractions away from the here and now. This was this . . . and nothing else. He felt Melisa tighten her embrace as if she were trying to penetrate his thoughts. He heard himself say, "I am nothing."

The tonal sophistication of the music enveloped him. He felt beautiful . . . and far away from insanity.

"I love you, Rick."

The words pierced him. But he was not frightened.

"I love you, too, Melisa. But . . . I only love you."

She seemed to understand what he was trying to imply. A tiny chill of disappointment altered her expression.

A musician with a small instrument case under his arm rushed past them to get out from under the rain. He invited them in.

They entered tentatively, feeling the weight of their clothes in these dry surroundings, and began to feel self-conscious about their appearance. The generous expressions and the creative eyes, however, made them feel at ease, again. Then Melisa broke free of him and disappeared into the crowded room.

Santo smoked all the marijuana that was passed to him and drank the free-flowing bourbon. He was higher than high, and the night flew by. Then, suddenly, the music stopped and he was invited to leave. Nobody told him he would have to face the night alone after taking a heavy hit of synthetic mescaline.

Nobody told him where Melisa had gone. Nobody had wanted him anymore.

He found himself standing outside in the middle of the street.

Suddenly, it had all gone bad.

The music was in his head and nowhere else. There . . . that brick house with the arched doorway . . . that's where he came from, wasn't it?

He walked toward it and, as he came within reach, he found himself back in the original starting spot in the middle of the street. He approached the house again and again and again, each time it was the same; the exact same repositioning, as if he were on a treadmill. He couldn't scream!

He looked at the white line on the center of the street and followed it to that distant point: eternity. He was forever alone: completely . . . and for eternity. He couldn't move. He looked down at his feet and saw broken glass and dirty cigarette butts.

What had he done to himself? What was he becoming? What had he become?

There was no place he could go. He was on the white line, and at the end of the line, approaching rock bottom. From here, there was only death.

He heard himself scream more than once and then again and again, until he felt the hands of restraint and the pressure of a flat gritty surface against his face. Then he heard the words, "Hold him down!" pierce into his uncertain consciousness.

"You taking drugs, boy? LSD?"

Their voices faded in and out without warning:

". . . wallet . . . bad trip . . . these kids . . . he's yours . . ."

His senses were strobing. But he realized he was at a police station. Then a moment of relative calm allowed him to discern one coherent exchange between two cops.

"Hey, this guy is a Vietnam vet. Look at these citations in his wallet: Silver Star, Bronze Star, Purple . . . hey, this guy's alright. What do you think?"

"Let's let him go."

"Yeah, let's."

"The poor bastard."

Julian was waiting in the lobby to receive him. Julian, good old Julian; he had enough soul left in him to put himself in jeopardy by entering a police station. He assured Santo everything was going to be alright. And he assured the officers that their halfway house was equipped to deal with these problems.

Kerry was waiting outside to help. Kerry, good old Kerry.

Santo crumbled when he felt the security of their support on both sides. But they didn't let him fall. Then they walked around the corner where Nat was waiting in his car. Nat. Good old . . . they packaged him into the back seat of the Chevrolet.

The next thing he felt was the motion of the car, which almost made him sick. But Kerry encouraged him to sit up and lean against the car door. The fresh air blowing on him through the window made him feel better.

"What the hell did you take, man?" Julian asked. He was nervously stroking his black beard.

"Bad . . . stuff."

They laughed.

"No shit."

Santo noticed the cowboy hat behind the driver's wheel. "Don't you ever . . . take off . . . that cowboy hat?"

They laughed, again. They were relieved.

Then Santo had enough strength to ask one more question. "What happened to Melisa?"

He heard voices:

"She's alright."

"Gladys is taking care of her."

"It's a good thing she was able to tell us what happened to you."

Santo began sinking into the blackness of a sleepless sleep that had no dreams. The last thing he heard was Kerry's disengaging voice and his gentle touch.

"They're both going to be alright."

Chapter 31

Utterly and Completely

Blue light filtered through the bedsheets hanging as drapes on rusty curtain rods. Both windows were located at the center of their adjacent walls, ninety degrees from each other. This had been Paisley and Gladys's, or rather—what was he doing here? he wondered. Then he remembered the bad mescaline and Julian and Kerry and Nat.

This bedroom was the farthest room from the rest of the house and, therefore, the quietest. It could have been any day and any time of day. He took a deep breath and exhaled slowly.

He felt as empty as this room, as burned out as he had ever been in his life. He was tired: utterly and completely. And he was afraid to remember what had happened to him because he was afraid of reactivating those frightening hallucinations; the tremors from the mescaline, or whatever he had snorted, still kept him on the fringes of terror.

He succumbed to a sudden burst of depression and felt a strong desire to cry, even though he couldn't. He found the strength instead to roll over on his back toward the center of the mattress, where he bumped into Melisa. She was awake. Her eyes glowed dimly, and she stared lifelessly at the ceiling without blinking.

All this and more he gathered from his peripheral vision. All this and more was all the strength he had left. He dozed off, momentarily.

"You alright?"

"What's alright?" Her voice was as breathy with exhaustion as his.

"Bad stuff," he said.

"Yeah."

There was a long interval of rest between each exchange that was comparable to the recharging of a battery long enough to transmit what was necessary before it completely discharged itself again.

"You disappeared."

"Almost forever," she muttered.

Birds chirped. A dog barked in the distance.

"I'm sorry."

"You're silly," she chided.

Then another kind of darkness gradually enveloped him into a black-and-white world of dreamless dreams that required his surrender. This was not courageous, it was necessary. He floated in this black-and-white world until he gained his footing. Then he looked down and realized he was standing on the roof of Six-thirteen, a place he no longer belonged. He stepped near the roof's edge and leaped into the colorless expanse, where he turned into a butterfly. He was free and filled with joy as he zigged and zagged and . . .

Filtered blue light awakened him. This time he knew it was a morning light. He sat up on the mattress, feeling weary of convalescence.

His movement stirred Melisa. She also sat up.

They stretched to relieve the muscular discomfort caused by their lengthy immobility. Their bones cracked.

"I feel dead."

"I am dead," he said.

She leaned toward him until she fell into his lap. "God. Never. Again."

"Never." He knew he meant what he said. He had used and abused himself with drugs during and since the war and realized he had had enough.

"Are you alright?" she asked. "I felt you shiver."

"I thought that was you." They laughed. "I was just thinking."

"About what?"

"About the number of times I've faced death."

"And?"

"And . . . there's no reason why I should be alive right now."

"Who needs a reason?"

"It's time."

"For what?"

"To be thankful."

She rolled off his lap. "Is that all?"

"Well . . . it's news to me," he said defensively.

"I'm sorry, I didn't mean to sound so cynical."

"But that's how you feel."

"I don't know what I feel," she said flatly. "Last night's insanity was just a reflection of what my life has been and what it plans to be. It doesn't matter if it ends today or tomorrow. I'm something to be used . . . until I'm used up. I'm only a whore."

"I'm sorry."

"Don't. You'll regret the sympathy you give me. Hold me. Just . . . hold me."

She fell into his lap again and she directed his arms around her. It made him wonder at what level she was trying to manipulate him this time. Then he became angry with himself over his suspicious nature.

Why did he always see the shadow of things and not the things themselves? Why did he always feel the shadow of an emotion and not the emotion itself?

He was tired of treating everybody like the enemy. Santo closed his eyes and saw a vision:

Dirt and debris. A dispirited woman. Her forehead pressed against a gray wall. Her outstretched hands encircling nothing.

The shades of blue became more intense as the sun rose higher in the sky. And the morning's coolness burned off, leaving a humidity that threatened to get worse. They finally left the safety of their bed and tentatively walked into the hallway together where they heard laughter. Then they assisted each other down the hallway, past the kitchen, through the living room, and into the front porch. Kerry was the first one to notice them.

"Welcome back to the world. It's only been two days."

Melisa's expression remained bland.

"I'm hungry," Santo said.

"Then how about breakfast?" And with Julian's assistance, Kerry ushered them into the kitchen.

"Are you two alright?" Julian asked.

"We're fine. Really."

"Is there any coffee made?"

"Coming right up, Richard."

"Where's Gladys?" Melisa asked.

"Out goofing with Nat," Julian said.

The coffee was heaven. It was the pick-up they needed to help them out of some of their depression. But the food didn't settle well in Santo's stomach. And judging by Melisa's expression, she was experiencing the same difficulty. They nursed a second cup of coffee in an attempt to keep their food down.

"Nat is beginning to get restless."

The seriousness of Julian's voice brought Santo into the third dimension.

"You're going to need money, I know." Then he slipped back into a flat two-dimensionality. He felt hollow more than he felt sick.

"Yeah, that same old story," Julian confessed.

"Tell him to stop worrying. I've got enough to get you all out of town."

"Aren't you coming?" Melisa said achromatically.

He ignored her.

"How much is enough?" Julian asked.

"About five hundred dollars."

"Alright, my man . . . my main man! Where'd you get it?"

"Off that Manford character. I hid it in our attic that night."

Julian's face beamed. "That's my man. Always thinking."

"We split the money so everybody gets seventy-five bucks and change."

"I'm not going anywhere," Kerry said.

"So. Neither am I. Everybody gets an equal share just the same." He saw Melisa frown with disappointment and interrupted her before she had a chance to launch an appeal. "Later, Melisa. We'll talk about it, later. Please."

Her intense expression deflated, but her hope remained intact.

"I'm going to miss you, Richard," Kerry said appreciatively.

"We'll stay in touch," Santo said.

"No. You can fool yourself, but not me. You're a loner, Richard—a misfit—but a nice one. Oh, sure, we'll see each other again once, maybe twice. But then the demands of our separate lives will . . . well, change us; make us travel different paths with . . . no intersections."

"Isn't that sweet," Melisa said bitterly. She rose from the kitchen table and walked unsteadily toward the door leading into the hallway. "I don't trust all this honesty and benevolence."

Santo stood up to make level eye contact with her. "I've never lied to you, Melisa."

"You've never told me the truth, either," she said caustically.

"Well . . . I'm not sure what that is, right now." He didn't want to hurt her. "Let's talk about this later. Please."

The rancor in her facial expression could be heard in the tone of her voice. "Sure. Later." Then she wobbled down the hallway and disappeared into the back room.

"She'll be alright," Kerry said. "I know how she feels."

"We split the money up tonight, alright?"

"Tonight," Julian agreed.

Santo felt the weight of his exhaustion, again. "I'm tired. I'm going to lie down."

"Make it good with her, man," Julian said when Santo reached the hallway door. "We're breaking this up tomorrow."

"Okay."

"It's going to be Nat and Gladys, Julian and Melisa. Have any problem with that?"

"Should I?"

"We'll have a big party tonight," Kerry said nervously.

"Relax, Kerry, baby. We're all big boys. Nothing happens until the four of us are on the road in the morning. Is that okay with you, Rick?"

"She's a grown woman."

"Yeah."

Santo turned away and shuffled down the hallway. He listened to Julian and Kerry as he hesitated at the bedroom door.

"Kerry. It sure would make it easier between us if I were a faggot."

"Well," Kerry said, "nobody's perfect."

They laughed because it was something good to do.

Santo remained standing there, trying to figure out what to say to Melisa. Then he realized he also had to figure out how. He hoped she was already asleep.

He ran his fingers through his hair. They trembled from the effects of his raw feelings that, although made from pure ingredients, were left unmixed in a bowl. He had nothing to offer a woman right now. He had nothing to offer anyone—not even himself.

Sleep. He needed more sleep. The intensity of these emotions had drained him to exhaustion.

CHAPTER 32

Sydney, Australia

His head was still throbbing from the pain of his wound. Rick leaned back against the bulkhead, feeling the weight of exhaustion envelop him. Then he angled toward the window and let the harsh wind blow against his face to help wipe away one set of memories for another.

The chopper banked to the right, momentarily, revealing the South China Sea again.

His mind drifted until he was somewhere else: in another lifetime—a million miles away from the war; in another lifetime—at Sydney, Australia.

He was lucky to get that R & R. It came at a time when he was beginning to worry about death . . . and that always meant death. He managed to survive a streak of bad-luck patrols with high casualty rates and aborted missions. But the stress was beginning to push him beyond the limit of his endurance.

The available R & R slot to Australia was a gift, which he grabbed with both hands. It broke the pattern of his despair.

His affair with Milly was uncommonly soft, strangely private, and intensely intimate. He was nursing a cup of coffee at a downtown diner, feeling lost in his new surroundings, when she sat next to him and laid a bill on the counter.

"Buy you another cup there, Yank?"

"Sure," he said.

"You're here from the war," she told him.

"Of course."

"Two coffees, please," she said to the waitress. She was extremely self-confident.

She opened her purse for her cigarettes, carefully guarding her green eyes from his; this was a delicate time between two strangers, no matter how willing.

He studied her as she went through the motions of lighting her cigarette: fair-skinned, shapely figure, auburn hair that flowed down her back like a shiny silk rug. She was striking but not beautiful; her small features were deprived of their perfection because of a cherry round nose and a vertical hairline scar near the center of her upper lip.

She exhaled the smoke from her deeply drawn cigarette. "My name's Milly."

"I'm Rick."

"You have very nice eyes for a soldier."

Rick lit a cigarette. He was at a loss for words. He was grateful when the waitress arrived with their coffee.

"Sugar?"

"You have five days."

"Yes," he said guardedly.

"Two sugars, please."

"You live here in Sydney?"

"Of course. Cream?"

"Sure."

"And you?"

"Does it matter?"

"Of course."

"Miami."

"Oh. The Sunshine State."

"I guess."

"You're young."

"So are you."

"Aren't we."

They continued talking until they began to laugh. Then she collected herself into a neat package and got up from her stool.

"Come on. You Tarzan, me Jane. I don't live far from here."

He picked up his small canvas bag and followed her out.

It was a beautiful day and this was a modern city. Rick always felt comfortable in a city . . . any city. They were always the same: filled with the colorful activity of people and traffic. He was happy to be in civilization again.

The sign on the street corner said William Street. But he was hopelessly lost. She stepped up the pace.

"Where are we going?"

"Near King's Cross," she said.

"Oh."

He continued following her, unable to focus on any one thing and content to stay within the blur of colors and movement and urban intensity.

They stopped in front of a simple, white stone apartment building. She started fishing for her keys.

"I've got to get a new purse," she said. "I can't ever find anything in it."

Exasperated, she went into the building, with Rick following her like a child. She found her keys after they reached the second floor of the modest, but clean, tenement.

When they entered her orderly two-room apartment, he felt the deliberate absence of a child. Everywhere he turned he saw the evidence of his existence: toys, second bed, a boy's clothes, even a cowboy hat and a six-shooter.

She turned to him and made the only demand she would ever ask of him. "Please, no bars, and . . . no past." She never mentioned, and he never asked about, the child. And with a gentle kiss, the tension of the last few months in the bush disappeared.

Their five days together were wonderful. He'd never lived with a woman before. It was very different from the one-night stands and cheap motel room shack-ups he'd known. The closest thing he'd ever come to this was Aurora. But her world was so completely different from his that there was never any hope for more than the intimacy of sex and food.

Milly was a quantum leap toward the understanding of a woman—something he knew very little about. And Milly engaged him in conversation, which made this a relationship. Together, they created an intimate world that suspended time and place in such a manner that he felt as if he belonged. They talked, with laughter and kisses, about everything—except *the war* in his life and *the man* in hers.

But on their fourth night together, she slipped and broke this unofficial rule. And in a manner that could have only come from years of drinking alone, she tossed down countless shots of Scotch at the kitchenette table.

He didn't have to confirm her drinking problem. He knew there were half-full and half-empty bottles hidden all over the apartment.

He stayed with her through the night, careful of his own drinking. And when she finally got to the point where she couldn't toss down another shot, she lifted her head from her unfocused stupor and cried, "This goddamn war!" and passed out.

He carried her to the bedroom and carefully placed her on the clean, white bed. He slept on the sofa that night.

She had breakfast ready when he woke up that following morning. She was pleasant and beautiful and attentive.

"Today is your last day. We must make it special. Yes?"

"Yes. And don't forget about tonight," he teased.

She draped a napkin suggestively over his face. "Don't worry about that, love. I won't."

They spent the day in familiar places, which made Rick feel more like a native. Then he wondered if this was Milly's usual wrap-up with a man: reality was creeping in.

The day went by too swiftly. But there was no way of holding onto it. And as their relationship began approaching its mortal end, Rick felt his old tensions return.

Milly noticed the change when he became impatient with a waiter. "Easy love, there's no use in all that."

"Yeah. I know. You're right."

"Maybe."

But the tension remained with him throughout the night. He was going back to the war and only Milly's calm demeanor was keeping the future from pouring in.

That night, he couldn't sleep or smoke or engage very passionately with Milly. He finally reached for his wallet on the bedside table and stripped it clean of all but a few bills. Then he cleared his throat after an awkward silence. "Milly."

"Yes?"

"Here. I want you to have this." He carefully folded her hand over the wad of bills.

"No, Rick. Don't."

"Shut up and take it."

"But . . ."

"Please. Take it."

"But . . . you don't need to . . . to . . ."

"That's right. I don't need it where I'm going. Believe me. Take it. Spend it on your . . . " but he stopped himself from saying, *your kid,* feeling embarrassed by his presumptuous invasion of her private life.

"That's alright, Rick." Her gentle touch supported what she said.

"Yeah. Sure. Buy yourself a purse."

"I will."

"Good. Let's try to get some sleep."

She leaned over and kissed him lightly on the lips before snuggling affectionately against his side. Rick tried to slip into a pleasant dream but he slipped into the harsh wind of reality instead.

Bearcat nudged him. "We're almost home!" Then he pointed to his M-16, signifying it was time to unload.

Rick mechanically pulled out the magazine and ejected the single round left in its chamber. And as soon as they started approaching their LZ, they slung their backpacks on and gathered the extra gear and weapons left by the wounded.

CHAPTER 33

All Mixed Up

Santo opened his eyes and stared at the bedroom ceiling. His limbs were stiff, and his joints ached from too much sleep. And when he stretched, he discovered Melisa was gone. He rolled toward the edge of the mattress and studied a dull chink of light passing through a small tear in one of the bedsheet drapes.

Dusk. He had slept through two-and-a-half days.

Then he caught sight of a pack of cigarettes and a box of matches with the corner of his eye. He snatched them off the floor and sat up on the edge of the mattress, noting that the bedroom door had been left open.

The smoke tasted good. And sitting felt good. So, he remained in this position until he smoked the cigarette to the filter. Then he let himself fall back into the mattress, leaving his knees bent and his feet flat on the floor. He stared at the cracked ceiling without focus and waited for distant thoughts. But there was no pursuit and no lingering. Random thoughts appeared and disappeared freely. Then a surge of energy propelled him into a vision:

A door appeared before him, cracked open a few inches, and released bright chinks of light from its vertical and two horizontal edges. Then a butterfly zigzagged toward the top vertical opening of the door and disappeared into the freedom of that mysterious chink of light.

A feeling of well-being began to consume him and put an end to his inner chaos; his thoughts became quiet and unified and . . . clear . . . that was it, clear! He sat up again: he knew his Six-thirteen life was almost over and everything was going to be alright. He knew! And in a humble revelation supported by three fragments of reality, he whispered timidly to himself: "I've got my life. I've got the G.I. Bill. I've got . . . a reason to stay." He collapsed into the mattress, again, startled by this simple insight and decision.

He broke into a cold sweat, which reminded him of that strange experience he had at the Conradi Theatre. Suddenly, he saw the stark darkness, connecting the past with his present, begin to brighten. He was not the same.

Then voices interrupted his reverie. He focused his attention until the voices and activity from the other bedroom clearly intruded on his senses.

It was Gladys and Melisa. And the door to the other bedroom was also open.

"I've got jobs waiting for us in Atlanta, Mel."

"God . . . I don't want to start turning tricks, again."

"Have you got a better idea? That seventy-five bucks Rick told you about isn't going to take us very far. Honey. I could use a friend with me."

There was a long silence.

"My life. I'm going nowhere fast with it."

"It won't be forever," Gladys assured. "We can pool our money."

"And do what?"

"Save it."

He heard the scrape of a chair followed by one of them walking heavily across the room. Gladys was sympathetic.

"You've got to forget about these guys, Mel."

"What about Nat?"

"He's nothing to me. They're losers."

"And what does that make us?"

Her challenge forced Gladys to be more aggressive.

"Alright. Go on and feel sorry for your goddamn self. Nobody's going to care. As for myself, I'm packing my bags and I'm going to load them into Nat's car. I'm leaving in the morning, with or without you."

Santo heard Gladys throwing her things together.

"I'm sorry, Gladys." But the activity continued as if Gladys was ignoring her. "I'm just so tired of it all."

The activity stopped. "I understand, honey. We're all mixed up. That doesn't make any of us bad. We just don't know . . . what we're doing."

"I simply want to stop running. I'm getting fed up with all these major changes in my life."

"Life is change, hon. There's nothing we can do about that. And as for running, well . . . stop running. Dig in and fight for your life."

"But . . . that's so hard to do."

"I didn't say it was going to be easy. Why the hell do you think I'm packing? Because life always looks greener when life looks new. I'm a coward. And . . . I know someday it's going to catch up with me." Gladys's voice dropped a full octave. "In the end . . . I know I'm doomed."

A long silence followed.

"Where will we live?" Melisa asked without conviction.

"Now you're talking, Mel. Come on, start packing. That's movement. And movement is good."

"I wish I had your confidence."

The activity in the room increased appreciably.

"That's nothing but a smoke screen," Gladys confessed. "Forget him, Mel. I almost went for him myself."

"I've got to try one more time before we leave in the morning. I can't help it."

"Crap. Then do it. I only wish I could save you the pain."

Santo stood up and quietly shut the door. It reduced the clarity of their activity and what remained of their conversation. Then Nat intruded on their privacy. He offered them his assistance.

Shortly thereafter, Santo heard luggage thumping against the doorjamb as Nat entered the hallway. He was carrying their bags. Santo stood by the closed door, listening.

He waited for them to go outside and finish loading their stuff into the trunk of Nat's car before he dragged himself down the hallway and into the bathroom. All he wanted to do was take a shower. He didn't want to face Melisa again, because he didn't want to hurt her. There was nothing noble about hurting somebody already wounded.

Cold water from a mildew-encrusted shower head washed his thoughts away.

CHAPTER 34

Friends

Gladys raised her glass of wine. "To Six-thirteen. May its people find serenity."

The sound of clinking glasses at the end of the toast penetrated the stillness of the house.

It had been a quiet party: without music and, except for a little marijuana Julian managed to acquire, without hard drugs. Cigarette smoke hung thickly above the candlelit atmosphere.

"I'm beginning to feel like we're camping out in this place," Gladys said. "No lights, no hot water, no sounds to listen to . . . Christ. I'd be happy with a transistor radio."

"Stop complaining," Nat said. "We could be stuck out there in the rain, sitting in my car."

"We can always go to my place," Kerry suggested.

"You're looking to get us into trouble and you evicted from there if you keep it up. I don't think they were bluffing when they chased us out of your room yesterday."

"Well, if you all wouldn't be so damn rowdy."

"Hey, we are what we are," Nat said. "Besides, they'll stop you the minute they see the six of us approach the lobby."

"You're my friends, and it's my place," Kerry said.

"I'm on your side, man. You don't have to preach to the choir. All I can say is look at us: we're not the leading citizens of Tallahassee. And if you keep it up, it's not going to be your place any longer."

"Then it's 'welcome to Atlanta' for you, too," Julian said.

The girls laughed nervously.

"I'm not so sure that's a bad idea. That is," Kerry added, "if you'd have me."

"Of course we would," Nat said. "You're one of us, no matter how cramped the car gets and no matter what kind of hardship it causes."

"That's right," Julian said. "No hardship is too great to face for a friend. It's share and share alike."

"You guys. I couldn't do that to you. You're my friends."

Santo felt sorry for Kerry and almost interfered. But he didn't have either the inclination or the strength. He caught Melisa studying him. He wondered what she saw. Then he shifted his attention back to Kerry, who was reaching into his pocket. Kerry was filled with gratitude.

"I can't go with my friends because I know I shouldn't. I haven't got much going in this town, but at least I have a part-time job as a female impersonator at the Apalachee A-Go-Go. Who knows, maybe I'll get a break into show business."

"And don't forget us when you do," Nat said sanctimoniously, as he watched Kerry pull out his share of the money that Santo had divided among them.

"Here. I want you all to have this, Nat."

"What are you doing?"

"I really don't need this money."

Nat's face twisted into a hypocritical expression that bordered on overacting. "No. I won't hear of it."

Julian snatched the money out of Kerry's hand. "Thank you, Kerry, baby . . . from the bottom of all our hearts. Right, Nathew?"

The animation in Nat's expression flattened because of Julian's decisive act. He hooked the fish but Julian got the prize.

"Yeah . . . sure . . . thanks, Kerry."

Santo was glad Kerry wasn't going to Atlanta with them; he'd gotten off cheap. But he couldn't bear to witness any more of this. He felt an anxious hand grip his forearm after he rose from his chair.

"We need to be alone," Melisa said openly.

There were no secrets here. The others knew what was at stake between them. If they decided to stay together, Julian would be without a woman, Gladys would lose a dependable comrade, and Nat would have to deal with two malcontents. They would also be seventy-five dollars poorer.

"Alright," Santo said. But before he followed her into their bedroom, he addressed the others. "If I don't see you all in the morning, take care of yourselves. I guess . . . well . . . we'll probably never see each other again."

None of them refuted his statement with sentimentality. But when he left the kitchen, he heard Kerry announce, "I'm going to give Richard a complimentary ticket to my very next show."

As soon as he shut the bedroom door, Melisa hovered close to him with a suffocating solicitude. He gently broke away from her and withheld his emotions.

"What's the matter?" she asked.

"Nothing."

"Then why are you avoiding me?"

"Stop playing games, Melisa."

She pursed her lips defiantly. "I'm not playing."

He ran his fingers through his hair and sighed. "I know. I'm sorry."

A nervous smile erased her defiant expression. "Gladys is my only friend."

"She's a fine lady."

She approached him from behind and gave him a hug. "Our candle is about to go out."

"There's another one by the bed, over there."

"Is that all there is? Is that all we have left?"

"I think so," he whispered delicately. "Yes," he said with finality.

She released him, found the fresh candle, and picked it up. And by the light of the sputtering flame, she twisted it into the opening of an empty wine bottle. She studied the object.

"I guess some people don't even get this much . . . the length of a candle."

"I'm sorry."

"Don't be." She lit the new candle and blew out the old one. "Done." She kissed him once, twice, three times, then until she got a response. Their feelings overflowed: they made love for the last time.

Afterwards, they were physically and emotionally spent. A long silence preceded Melisa's final appeal.

"I don't want to go with Gladys to Atlanta. I require very little. You see that, don't you?"

He caressed her without answering the question.

He didn't love her. And whether she knew it or not, she didn't love him. A single tear grudgingly trickled down the left side of her face. He was moved by its sincerity.

"I can't help you, Melisa. I can't even help myself, yet."

She snuggled closely to him and remained tender. He reciprocated, in a detached manner, and together they listened to the muted activity taking place in the house.

"The war has cut the heart out of me. And with it, my ability to love in the way you want me to love. I think . . . that makes me a casualty. Shit, that sounds stupid, I know."

"No . . . no, it doesn't."

"You're a fine person. But . . . I can't . . . I don't know . . . I'm not ready."

She broke away from him and lit a cigarette, which they shared. Its orange point, along with the flickering candle, was the only thing that gave meaning and life to the bedroom's darkness.

CHAPTER 35

Remember When

Santo woke up coughing. His sinuses burned and he was blind—he smelled smoke. Then he heard a distant cry: "Fire!"

Melisa was not asleep; she was unconscious. He shook her into a semi-comatose condition, which began with a cough. She gasped for clean air. Then she cried out in a panic. She attempted to rise from the mattress, but all she managed to do was roll onto the floor and start choking.

He reached into the blackness and grabbed her by the arm, but then he let her go. He didn't want to leave her, but he had to quickly find an avenue of escape because he was also gasping heavily and beginning to feel dizzy from the toxic fumes.

He crawled to the door. It felt hot. He knew he shouldn't but he had to take a chance and open the door. When he did, he felt heat and smoke roll in above him. Then he saw the glow of the fire. He slammed the door shut. He knew there was no escape there and little time left.

He groped his way along the wall until he reached one of the windows and pulled the bedsheet off the curtain rod. The window was open, and the only thing obstructing their way out was the window's screen.

He had to hurry. The smoke and the toxic gases were becoming unbearable. Melisa was no longer coughing.

He kept his head. He followed the edge of the screen with his hands and unlocked enough holding latches for him to forcefully pull the screen off the window casing. Then he turned to get Melisa and tripped over the bedsheet. He rose, tied the bedsheet around him like a skirt, and felt his way back to the mattress. His eyes, nose, throat, and chest were screaming with pain.

He finally located Melisa. She was curled up in a ball and unconscious. He slung her over his right shoulder and stumbled about the room until he located the open window again. She weighed a ton; he weighed a ton.

He slumped against the window casing, panting and wheezing and doubting whether he could successfully lower her out through the opening. He had to hurry. Seconds were becoming precious.

He pulled the bedsheet from his waist and dropped it over the windowsill. And with great effort, he lowered her naked body from his shoulder and slid her through the window, feet first, until he was left holding her under each armpit. As soon as her head cleared, he let her drop to the ground. Then he straddled the window, lifted his inside leg over, and jumped out.

He stood up and yanked the bedsheet from the windowsill. Then, in an effort to gulp down clean air, he choked and frothed and spat and slung away the mucus running down his nose with the back of his hand. He wanted to get on his knees and cough until he felt better, but he knew Melisa needed medical attention.

He rolled her onto her back and discovered she wasn't breathing. But she had a pulse. He opened her mouth and hyperextended her neck to make sure she had a clear airway. Then he placed his mouth over hers, pinched her nose shut, and blew several breaths into her. But the pain in his own chest prevented those breaths from being very strong. He continued to push himself beyond his endurance, however, and gave her whatever air he had.

Suddenly, liquid gurgled into her mouth as she convulsed. Then she rolled onto her side into a ball and gulped spasmodically for air as she vomited.

He plopped onto the ground beside her, totally exhausted. But he knew she was going to be alright: he heard her crying. Then he looked up and saw flames appear through their window. The fire was rapidly consuming old Six-thirteen.

"My God, I hope everybody got out," he said. But she was too weak to respond.

He stood up, wrapped the bedsheet around his waist, then carried Melisa away from the fully involved house fire to the far side of the backyard. Then he draped a discarded piece of shag carpet over her that he found nearby. He heard sirens in the distance.

"Don't move. You're going to be alright. I'll let the paramedics know you're back here. Don't move. Do you understand?"

She nodded her head.

He tightened the bedsheet around his waist and went to the front of the house. An ambulance drove up just as he reached the sidewalk. Two paramedics jumped out of the vehicle and approached him.

"I'm alright, I'm alright. But there's a lady in the backyard that needs attention. She's breathing . . . and she's awake."

The paramedics brushed past him in the direction he was pointing, carrying an oxygen bottle and other first aid equipment.

The lights and sounds of fire engines had flooded the entire street in a deluge of machinery and men. The activity was so overwhelming and frightening that he became concerned about the others again. He turned toward the house to start looking for them and caught sight of two figures, Nat and Gladys, covering their nakedness by sharing a bedsheet. He ran over to them.

"You guys alright?"

"You don't have to worry about us," Nat said.

"Melisa . . ."

"She's alright, Gladys. She's in the backyard. Have you seen Julian and Kerry?"

"No."

"Where were they?"

"Last thing I can remember, they were on the front porch," Nat said.

"What the hell happened?"

"I don't know, Rick. Candles, Sterno, cigarettes . . . we all fell asleep. One of them got us."

Several firefighters rushed past them to fight the blaze. One of them stopped. "I'm going to have to ask you all to stand aside. You're better off across the street. Please."

The house was being consumed.

"My God," Santo said, "if they're in there."

"Who's in there?" the firefighter said. "You mean there's somebody still in there?"

"Two," Santo said. "I think."

The firefighter quickly left them and rushed toward the other firefighters with this information. His concern infected Santo to such a degree that he ran along the other side of the house, calling for them until he heard a familiar voice. He saw Julian.

"Are you alright?"

"I think so," Julian said, coughing as if he had bronchitis.

"Where's Kerry?"

"How . . . how should I know?"

"He was with you, wasn't he?"

Julian nervously began tucking his tee shirt into his pants. "So?"

"He was with you, man!"

"I thought it was understood," he said defensively, "every man for himself." He coughed.

"Not here. Not at home! Julian . . . where is he?"

"Are those the two?" Santo heard a firefighter shout.

"I . . . I . . . don't know. I mean . . . he's in there . . . I guess. It ain't my fault," Julian said impotently. He coughed.

"Are you the two who were supposed to be in there?" a firefighter asked.

"One of them," Santo said, pointing at Julian. "The other one is still in there." Santo started walking toward the house.

"Where the hell are you going?" one of the firefighters said.

"After him."

"No you're not. That's what we're here for."

"Get out of my way. Kerry. Kerry!"

But the heat and the firefighters prevented Santo from going in. Then the firefighters escorted them across the street where they had taken the others.

The four of them huddled in and around Nat's car watching the inferno—knowing Kerry was in there. There were no words. No feelings. Until Julian began to cry.

"I'm sorry," Santo said. "I shouldn't have said . . . it wasn't your fault."

"No, man, you were right on. And now I'm . . . lost . . . forever . . . again."

"Crap. Stop that shit," Nat said. "Nobody's pointing a finger at you. Forget it!"

"I can't!" Julian exploded. "Sometimes the truth . . . is . . . the truth."

And because Nat didn't know what else to say, he filled the silence by opening the trunk and pulling out an odd assortment of jeans and shorts and tee shirts for those who needed clothes; there was no attempt at modesty while dressing under these conditions. Then Santo noticed Gladys's expression change as she stepped into a pair of shorts. He peered in the direction she was looking and saw a figure scurrying toward them. He was certain he recognized the waddle but he was afraid it was wishful thinking. He checked with Gladys again. She had a tee shirt pressed against her bosom.

"It's him," she said. "It's really him."

"Kerry." Santo ran toward him. "Kerry! It's really you!"

"I started running . . . as soon as . . . I could see . . . the fire," he said, as he tried to catch his breath.

"Where the hell have you been?" Gladys demanded. "You scared the hell out of us!" She hit him on the arm.

"Oww! I couldn't sleep. So, I went home to get a change of clothes." He showed them a pair of pants and a shirt on a wire hanger. "See?"

"Hey, what's going on?" Melisa wailed, as she hobbled across the street.

"Melisa!" Santo hurried over to her. She was draped in a sheet that the paramedics had given her. "How are you?"

She leaned against Santo and coughed. "I had enough oxygen."

Santo guided her alongside Nat's car. "Look, Melisa, it's Kerry."

Melisa glanced at Kerry before leaning against Santo for more support. "And?"

Kerry was bewildered. His ironed slacks slipped off the wire hanger. "Gosh, is everybody alright?"

"Yeah," Julian said. "Everybody's alright, now. Come here." Julian caressed him with a sincerity that took Kerry by surprise.

"My, my. Maybe I should take up arson for a hobby."

Everybody laughed because laughter was all that was left in them.

Cloaked under one another's shadow, Six-thirteen became a memory in the minds of six people as it burned to the ground. They were Six-thirteen, now . . . changed, yet unchanged; because everything existed in relation to everything else. Kerry was less bitter, Melisa less plain, Julian less satanic, Nat less cruel, Gladys less cynical, and Rick less confused. They'd become a different band of outcasts.

They were interrogated by the police and the fire department until the investigators were satisfied that the cause of the fire was an accident. Then they lost interest in the motley group.

"Thanks again for the money, Rick," Gladys said.

"Sure. It's a good thing you were already packed."

She nodded. "Yeah. Do you mind if we get cleaned up at your place before we leave for Atlanta, Kerry?"

"Please, be my guests."

"I don't want any more trouble in this damn town," Nat said. "So, if we're going to cause you any problems by going over to your place . . ."

"We'll go upstairs two at a time," Kerry said. "They can't complain about that."

"Okay then, let's go."

Gladys and Kerry joined Melisa, who was already sitting in the back seat. Julian sat in the front, while Nat took the wheel.

"Are you coming, Rick?"

"No. This is it for me."

"Come on, Richard. You can't go around town in a bedsheet."

"Thanks, Kerry. I've got clothes in the trunk of my car. And the rear floorboard has my extra key. I'll make out."

"Suit yourself then," Nat said, as he started his car. "Take care of yourself, partner."

As the car pulled away from the street curb, Melisa and Gladys looked at Rick through the rear window without expression. He responded with a half-hearted wave, reassuring himself that it was better . . . to remember when . . .

CHAPTER 36

Into the Face of Reality

They walked off the chopper in a single file and went straight to the yellow line where the armorers plucked from each man his leftover fragmentation, incendiary, white phosphorous, and colored smoke grenades, as they watched a sea of outgoing patrols get underway. And because there was laughter and corny jokes and cautious inquiries about the missing men, this was a relatively pleasant time for an incoming patrol.

"Anybody get wasted?"

"No: three got wounded."

"Was Kafka with you guys?"

"Yeah."

"He got it in the gut."

"Bad news. Is he going to make it?"

"Who knows."

"He was the best M-79 man in the battalion."

"Yeah."

"He'll be okay."

"Damn right."

Then they were asked about the other two wounded guys. It was like talking to distant relatives who were deeply concerned yet carefully unemotional and objective. It was good to be home.

"Rick, I'll take the debrief," Russo said after the armorers finished stripping off his ordnance.

"You sure? I don't mind going."

Russo shrugged his shoulders. "I'll come get you if you're needed." Then he walked away in the direction of the Intell Center.

Rick joined the others on the long climb up the steep hill leading to their company area. They were looking forward to plenty of hot food, long showers, and a lot of cold beer; they had given up the practice of cleaning their gear immediately after a patrol—that was stateside-duty mentality. So, when Rick got to his hooch, he dumped all his gear on his cot, stripped himself naked, and grabbed a beer from the hooch's mini-refrigerator instead. It was an outrageous luxury.

He popped open the beer and drank it until the cold hurt his head. Then he looked around, a bit disoriented by this painful pleasure, and began to laugh uncontrollably.

He grabbed a pack of cigarettes, lit a smoke, and went through the back door of the hooch to sit in his chair. He gently lowered himself onto the tattered chaise lounge because it felt good to gradually feel the sensation of the chair's fabric against his skin.

The sun was warm, the sky was blue, and the panorama of the rice paddies below was beautiful. He settled into his chair more comfortably and enjoyed the tingling sensation of blood circulation returning to his feet. Life was good.

With a lit cigarette in one hand and a cold beer in the other, he stretched his body to embrace the beautiful world with his feelings: this wasn't a dream. Then he relaxed and exhaled deeply as he looked directly into the face of reality without saying the words: *I made it. I made it. Again.*

Epilogue

Yesterday and a Wake-up

Thirteen months and a wake-up. That's where Rick found himself sixteen months ago in dusty Da Nang while awaiting transport to his new unit. The stunning reality of his exile from all things familiar was as unclearly defined to him then as it was for him now. Because for thirteen long months, he was an alien on his own planet, an experience that was going to influence the rest of his life.

There was a definite lack of commitment and a definite lack of believing in things, which made him deficient by society's standards. True, he was enrolled at Florida State University. True, he wasn't worried about money—he more than earned his G.I. Bill. And true, he didn't know what to do with his life.

Why didn't he care? Why wasn't he impressed by people and their values? And why did he feel like he was just going through the motions? Because maybe, he thought, staying in motion was the only thing he knew how to do.

Keep moving. Don't think. Survive.

Then he felt the weight of the canvas bag that was slung over his shoulder; he had to remind himself that it wasn't ammo or food or water—these were books! He remembered now: he was happy! He was free to put his life back together. Free to forget the dog faces . . . the sweat . . . the unexplainable . . . the eyes of the dead.

He accidentally bumped into another student and heard himself apologize, anticipating a rebuke. But he received an apology instead. The person treated him as an equal. An equal! He was back, and he was one of them. They couldn't see what the war had done to him. He looked like everybody else.

He was stunned by this realization.

He wasn't alone! The nightmare was over! Yesterday and a wake-up was here . . . and now! Nothing mattered! Because he was going to live . . . until he died.

He started walking as if he was leaving his past worlds behind him: the world before the war, the world of war, and the Six-thirteen world after the war. The war: it became a tolerable daydream that couldn't hurt him anymore because it made his life real; he was no longer afraid.

Click. The daydream turned into the specific sound of choppers overhead. He looked up into the sky as he approached the edge of Landis Green's giant water fountain. And despite the distant sound of small-arms fire, the sky was beautiful—there was no paranoia.

He knew nobody was watching him or even cared to watch him. These moments of gentle insanity were his alone; he no longer resisted them.

He dropped his canvas bookbag on the ground and plunged his cupped hands into the fountain's water for a drink. This had once been a bombed-out crater filled with stagnant water; he drank the water hoping to contract a disease that would get him medevac'd out of that life. Now, he drank the water to cleanse himself—to be medevac'd into this life. When he saw himself reflected on the fountain's surface, he plunged his cupped hands into the water again and splashed his face.

A young lady wearing shorts and wading in Landis Green's water fountain brought him back into the present. But he remained calm. Because he was alright . . . even though the war would always be with him: no regrets. Listen, the distance . . . and the sound of choppers: to cry, without a cry . . . tears.

He stepped into the fountain. The cool water lapped against his legs as he looked up into the bright blue sky and realized: he no longer dwelled in the kind of darkness that held no promise of a dawn.

D. S. Lliteras is the author of six novels and one book of haiku and photography based on his Vietnam War experiences. He is an MFA graduate of Florida State University and a retired professional firefighter. He lives with his wife, Kathleen, in Virginia Beach, Virginia.

Praise for *Judas the Gentile*

> "Subtle, provocative."
> —starred review, *Booklist*

> "A true work of enduring literature . . ."
> —*Wisconsin Bookwatch*

> "Enormously rewarding."
> —*The Virginian-Pilot*

Praise for *The Thieves of Golgotha*

> "Thought-provoking . . . Recommended."
> —*Library Journal*

> "A sympathetic fictional portrait."
> —*Publishers Weekly*

> "Startling, surprisingly successful . . ."
> —*Booklist*

Hampton Roads Publishing Company
publishes books on a variety of subjects including
metaphysics, health, complementary medicine,
visionary fiction, and other related topics.

For a copy of our latest catalog,
call toll-free, 800-766-8009,
or send your name and address to:

Hampton Roads Publishing Company, Inc.
1125 Stoney Ridge Road
Charlottesville, VA 22902
email: hrpc@hrpub.com
www.hrpub.com